"I still want to claim what's mine."

Nat's eyes glistened dangerously before he pulled her close and possessed her mouth.

Though Imogen's senses were outraged there was a sharp bittersweet feeling of recognition—a coming home as her body was firmly molded to his.

The kiss was soft and treacherously seductive. Nat's hands gently coaxed a response from her emotionally starved body, until the familiar heat raced through her.

Then suddenly panic struck. For three years Imogen had managed to forget him and in a pityingly few seconds her body had surrendered to the memory. Angrily she wrenched herself free.

"I hate you, Nat Beaumont! Why can't you just go away and stay out of my life?"

"That might be easier said than done," he murmured huskily.

The Trodden Paths

by

JACQUELINE GILBERT

Harlequin Books

TORONTO • LONDON • LOS ANGELES • AMSTERDAM
SYDNEY • HAMBURG • PARIS • STOCKHOLM • ATHENS • TOKYO

Original hardcover edition published in 1982
by Mills & Boon Limited

ISBN 0-373-02492-4

Harlequin Romance first edition August 1982

For my friend
JUDY

Rosalind: O, how full of briers is this working-day world!

Celia: They are but burrs, cousin, thrown upon thee
in holiday foolery; if we walk not in the trodden
paths, our very petticoats will catch them.

As You Like It
William Shakespeare

CHAPTER ONE

'They have their exits and their entrances'

IMOGEN ADAIR, sitting in the driver's seat of the silver-grey Rover, gave a brief glance at her father, next to her. Gerard Adair caught the movement out of the corner of his eye and turned his head and they exchanged a smile.

'All right, Pa?' Imogen asked, and Gerard nodded without replying. 'Not long now, with a bit of luck,' she promised, hoping she was right, for the line of traffic ahead seemed solid.

The sun, making a brave showing earlier, had not lasted on this first Sunday in March, and in the on-coming dusk the only splashes of colour were the few yellow daffodils and red tulips that were sprouting optimistically from concrete tubs down the centre of the road.

Imogen edged the Rover towards a gap between a taxi and a bus, smiling at the cabby as he waved her through. Driving was a chore she was able to do for her father. Most men, she knew, hated being driven by a woman, but not Gerard, who disliked anything mechanical and rarely drove, especially in London. Traffic jams, such as the one they were caught in now, tried his patience to the limit.

To take his mind off the delay, Imogen said cheerfully:

'Liz phoned this afternoon while you were resting to wish you luck. They have plans for going on after the show for a meal at that new place, The Oasis, I

7

think it's called. I'm looking forward to seeing Liz
and Adam again—wasn't it kind of them to think of
including me in their party?'

Gerard again nodded without speaking, but
Imogen was used to his silences before performing in
front of an audience. It was almost as if a metamor-
phosis was already beginning in his character long
before he donned his costume and walked on stage.

Slowing down for traffic lights, Imogen allowed
herself to dwell on the Carlyons. Liz and Adam had
always shown her kindness and she was deeply
attached to them both. She had not seen them
lately—the last time being at their daughter's chris-
tening—a travelling theatrical company was not
conducive to keeping in touch by person, but the
rapport between them was always strong when they
did manage to meet up. She began to hum under
her breath, and Gerard said suddenly:

'You sound happy,' and his voice was indulgent.

Imogen grinned, and said cheerfully: 'I do, don't
I? Well, life is good. What more could a girl ask
than to sit among friends and watch her pa perform
before Royalty? I'm proud and happy for you,
darling.'

Gerard waved this aside and murmured: 'It's just
another performance,' and Imogen laughed gently,
saying teasingly: 'You old fraud,' and saw her father
smile.

There was another reason for her happiness, although she felt slightly guilty about it—unnecessarily
so, but then guilt sprang from all sorts of unlikely
sources. Tomorrow, after she had driven Gerard to
Heathrow for his flight to America, she was to go on
to Queensbridge, the promise of some exciting work
ahead awaiting her under Adam's guiding hands.
How grand it will be, working for Adam, she thought

with pleasure. Having a famous actor/manager for a father meant that she rarely worked for anyone else, and Gerard Adair was slow in his praise regarding colleagues in the profession. He did voice his respect for Adam Carlyon, both as an artistic director and as a friend of many years' standing, and it was not difficult for Imogen to follow his lead, for she had hero-worshipped Adam since being a child.

She flicked her father another brief glance, taking in his smooth head of near-white hair, the patrician profile, the blue eyes and sensitive mouth. At fifty-eight he still cut a trim figure, Imogen decided with pride.

'Tired, Pa?' she asked, and Gerard considered the question.

'A little,' he admitted. 'Rehearsals this morning were mostly waiting around, which can be wearying, as you know. However, the adrenalin will soon be flowing, giving me a new lease of life.'

Imogen said reflectively: 'It's funny how once you're on stage you forget all your aches and pains.' A memory struck her. 'Do you remember when I had 'flu once and went on without telling anyone how ill I was? To this day the whole performance is a complete blank, yet I got through it without turning a hair!' She grinned and intoned: 'The show must go on,' and Gerard smiled obligingly.

She glanced down at the dash clock, relieved to see they were in good time. Gerard always liked a period of quiet contemplation before going on, and as in everything else connected with the art of acting, Imogen had learned to copy him, realising the calming, beneficial effect it had.

They were now cruising past Trafalgar Square and Imogen's love of London made her blurt out longingly:

'It's a pity we can't base the Adair Company in

London, Pa,' and Gerard answered rather sharply:

'Not practical, my dear. Too risky and expensive.'

Imogen wrinkled her nose regretfully. She knew he was right. Their life-style had always been an up-and-down one, especially when she was young, but as her father's personal success had grown so had their digs and hotels improved. He never spoke of the financial side of their affairs, but Imogen was intelligent enough to realise that there was little security in their line of business.

Branching off St Martin's, Imogen noticed that the constabulary was out in force, waiting for the Royal car to pass later. It was getting more and more crowded as people and cars flocked towards the theatre and she was forced to slow down to a crawl.

'I'll leave the car keys at the stage door for Duggan to collect,' she announced, smiling through the rear-view mirror at the third person sitting silently and rather primly in the back. The faithful Duggan, Gerard's dresser, manservant, valet—Imogen could never make up her mind what to call him. So far as she could remember, Mortimer Duggan had been part of their lives always.

'You'll convey my apologies to Liz and Adam? Not seeing them afterwards,' Gerard prompted, as the dark blue columns of the Theatre Royal, Drury Lane, came into view.

'Yes, I will,' Imogen assured him, frowning slightly with concentration as she manoeuvred the narrow street. Billboards were propped up against the building, advertising 'One-Night Royal Gala Charity Performance'. Seeing them, she gave a shiver of excitement. She ignored the yellow lines and slowed the car to a halt, leaning across to brush her father's cheek with her lips, wondering at his composure and envying him it.

'Good luck, Pa,' she said fervently, and Gerard gave her his endearingly absent smile, lost in what lay ahead. Duggan, already out, opened the door for him and immediately a group broke away from the crowd by the foyer entrance and surrounded them, autograph books extended. A policeman strolled over, pointed a white-gloved hand at the yellow lines and Imogen beamed him an apology and moved on.

Having parked the car and handed in the keys, she entered the front foyer and enthusiastically breathed in the heady atmosphere that always pervaded any theatre, especially one harbouring such an auspicious occasion as this one tonight. Men in their evening suits and women in furs, long dresses and jewellery made their way, laughing and talking, past the photographs of the star-studded cast.

Imogen paused before the one of her father. It was one of her favourites, taken when he was playing Brutus, and the familiar feeling of pride rushed over her. She wanted to turn round and shout out—hey, folks, this is my pa!—and the impulse amused her, but she naturally denied it out of deference to her twenty-five years.

She deposited her short fur jacket in the cloakroom, bought a programme and made her way into the auditorium. It was alive with the buzz of conversation and she was halted once or twice on the way to her seat by friends of her father. By the time she had checked her ticket against the row, the orchestra was beginning to tune up.

Scanning the sea of faces Imogen saw that Liz and Adam were already seated, an empty place next to them gaping invitingly. She caught their eye and waved the programme in greeting and then began to make her way along the row to join them. Progress

was slow. She knew so many of the Carlyons' friends
and it was necessary to smile and say a word or two
on the way.

She had a nice smile. It was quick and ready,
warm and generous, flanked either side by two delightful dimples, and usually drew forth an immediate response from the recipient. There was also
something very appealing about the extremely large
grey eyes which were thickly fringed and tended to
sparkle when she smiled. It was, perhaps, the direct-
ness of the look, the honest interest held in their
depths and the way she had of tilting her head to
listen. Not a beautiful face, in the classic sense, but
an intelligent, attractive one, alive and full of
changing expression. Her smooth cap of dark brown
hair was shaped to suit the curve of her heart-shaped
face, and tonight it shone with special lustre, as if
she had taken extra pains with it. Her long gown of
wild silk, Orientally styled and patterned in richly
coloured blues and golds, heightened her pale,
creamy complexion and slim, youthful figure. There
was, tonight, an added glow to her, making her
especially noticeable. The grey eyes shone and the
smooth cheeks were rosy. Imogen knew that she was
looking her best and revelled in it. After all, it was
not every day that one's father was honoured by
being asked to perform before Royalty and she
thought it reasonable that a little of the euphoria
should rub off on to her. She was excited and elated,
and it showed.

At last she was nearly at her seat, breathless and
smiling. There was someone sitting in the one previous to her own, a man in evening suit, who, with his
head down and his eyes fixed on his programme,
had not noticed her passage along the row. Long
legs barred her way, and Imogen waited a moment

and then murmured:

'I'm so sorry to trouble you . . . will you excuse me, please?'

She had no premonition, no recognition in the downward turned head. Why should she have? There were many tall, fair-haired men sitting in the auditorium. It was a long time since the sight of such a one caused her heart to miss a beat, and we rarely see what we do not expect to see.

At her words the man's eyes lifted from the programme and without haste he rose to his feet to tower above her.

The smile of thanks already forming on her lips faltered and froze. The surrounding noise and activities receded into the background and she found herself drowning in the depths of familiar light green eyes which were gazing dispassionately down at her. The shock forced the blood to leave her face so rapidly that his hands came up to steady her.

Their touch galvanised her into action. With a quick gasp of breath, Imogen dragged her eyes away and forced herself to move on. As his hand dropped to push down her seat, she heard his polite: 'Allow me,' as though it came through a long tunnel.

She sank down with relief. She had forgotten how tall he was, how his slender fingers could encircle her bare arm. His voice was the same, deep and husky-velvet and, to her sensitive ears, now tinged with ironic amusement. Yes, he would find this meeting vastly diverting, she thought bitterly. He had always suffered a sardonic sense of humour and this unexpected confrontation would appeal to the quirky side of it.

As the surroundings bore down on Imogen once more she was beset by a jumble of disjointed questions that screamed around inside her head, making

it ache. What pleasantries she exchanged with her
friends, Liz and Adam Carlyon, seated on her other
side, she had no idea, but she must have been cohe-
rent and outwardly normal. Inside was another
matter. Inside was tumult and panic.

Mindful of his duties as host, Adam leaned forward slightly, his words and look embracing them
both.

'Imogen, I don't know whether you've met
Nathaniel Beaumont? He's just returned from
Australia, hence the attractive tan. Nat ... Imogen
Adair, actress in her own right, but also daughter of
Gerard Adair.'

Imogen was forced to turn from Adam and face
memories she had been trying for three years to
forget. She had thought she had succeeded, fool that
she was.

'Miss Adair and I have met before, Adam. Some
... three years ago, I believe ... a long time.' Nat
held out his hand. 'Too long,' he added smoothly.
'How are you, Imogen? You're looking extremely
well—delightful, in fact. And Gerard—I trust he's
also in the best of health?' The clasp of his hand was
brief.

Imogen unclamped her jaw and murmured a
noncommittal reply, and Adam went on:

'Of course, I should have guessed you'd know each
other. You've worked with Gerard, haven't you?'

'I've crossed swords with him more than once,'
Nat agreed, his eyes bright and slanting, his tone
ironical.

Imogen dropped her eyes to the programme and
pretended to be engrossed, trying to still the trembling of her hands. Every leaping sense in her body
was in screaming awareness of Nat, sitting by her
side, his arm resting on the ledge between them. How

could he sit there, so calm and composed, as if nothing had ever happened between them? As if they were almost strangers? A bitter lump stuck in her throat. That was just what they had been—intimate strangers!

The memory of that last, awful meeting, when she was all feelings and emotion and he had been icily contained and controlled, struck her, its imprint violent and harsh. Before it could snowball, the orchestra struck up the opening bars of the National Anthem as the Prince and Princess of Wales took their places, and Imogen rose to her feet with the rest of the audience, hardly aware of what was going on. When everyone was once more settled, the lights dimmed and the gala performance began.

Sitting tense and racked with emotion difficult to define, Imogen wished with all her heart that she could go back those few minutes—and it was only that, even though it felt an eternity—and meet Nat again. She had known that somewhere, some time she would have to come face to face with him once more, but she had hoped she would be able to meet him with cool impartiality and not with the overwhelming panic that had overtaken her. She was mortified. Her pride was stricken. She should be, and was, ashamed that this meeting could affect her so, especially as he had shown very clearly by his steady silence since they parted that he had wiped her right out of his life. He had made a decision and kept to it. A hard, determined man was Nathaniel Beaumont. A man who had no time for half-measures or divided loyalties.

Well, good luck to him, and he was right—they were not suited. But she was no longer the naïve and trusting Imogen that Nat had known. She had grown up in these past three years and not before time. She

had added a protective shell, a few layers of insula-
tion since then. So why had she gone to pieces the
minute she set eyes on him?

Because it was a shock, she told herself kindly.
Because when it came to the crunch she could not
wipe out completely the happy times, the exquisite
heights, the laughter they had shared together.
Surely one's first love was always something special,
would always have a small place in one's heart, even
when it did not last? she consoled herself valiantly,
aware that the protective shell was not so tough as
she had hoped.

The programme slipped from her fingers and
floated to the floor, landing sharply against Nat's
highly polished shoe. Before she could move, he had
bent to retrieve it. Vexed, Imogen felt her colour
deepen as she held out her hand to reclaim it and as
her fingers closed over it Nat still retained his grasp.
She glared at him. In the darkness of the theatre it
was difficult to make out his expression. The
wretched programme was surrendered and she
turned resolutely to the stage. He always did have
an odd sense of humour and she certainly did not
need reminding of his presence!

The first half seemed never-ending, but eventually
the curtain came down and the Carlyon party made
for the bar. Imogen ignored Nat as casually as she
could, noticing that Nat appeared to be completely
uninterested in her. Pride made it imperative that
she should enjoy herself, and she stretched her lips
into smiles and forced a sparkle to her eyes. It was a
commendable performance.

The bar was hot, noisy and crowded. Someone
nearby asked:

'How long have you been back in England, Nat?'
and Imogen, safe behind Adam, pricked up her ears.

'Three weeks.' Nat took a drink and grinned. 'You can't beat a pint of good old English beer!'

'And are you thinking of emigrating to Australia?' quizzed Liz.

'No, Lizzie, my dear—too many roots here, but it's a fascinating country and has tremendous scope in our field. I'd like to go back again some time.' He quirked a brow. 'It's funny—it wasn't until I was savouring the full blast of the biting East Coast wind and watched the grey waves of the North Sea pounding on the shore that I realised just how much I'd missed the place.' He grinned. 'Even the climate!'

Someone else said: 'You've made a hit with the critics for your work over there, Beaumont. Are you intending shaking up the film industry here as well?'

'I've had offers,' Nat admitted, studying the liquid in his glass thoughtfully, 'but it's time for me to return to my first love, the theatre, for a spell.'

Talk became general and, absently sipping her drink, Imogen found her eyes drawn to Nat, unobserved behind Adam's back.

Three years, and he had not changed . . . if anything, it was a shock to see him so familiar. He had always been good to look at—she had a preference for tall, lean men with classical features, and the deep tan, a legacy from the Australian climate, suited him, and had turned his hair into sun-bleached streaks. The effete, almost indolent image he mostly affected was a misguided one, she knew, and was given emphasis by an immaculate, but moderate, sense of dress. Beneath the relaxed pose emanated a fit body and a vigorous energy, and behind the drawling façade was a razor-sharp intelligence. She only knew the professional Nat Beaumont by repute, the private one she had been allowed a glimpse.

She saw his head come down, a lock of hair falling across his forehead, as a striking redhead demanded his attention. The redhead's eyes were bold and a look of appraisal passed between them. No doubt, Imogen thought angrily, those expressive green eyes could still gleam with shared amusement, and those lips reduce some poor female to a jelly . . . but not this one! Oh, dear God, not this one!

The redhead whispered something in his ear that made Nat throw back his head and laugh. The second bell sounded, recalling patrons to their seats, and he swung round, placing his empty glass down on the bar top. The movement caught Imogen by surprise and she was unprepared when his eyes locked with hers. His glance barely faltered before passing on. Emotion clutched painfully at her throat. She downed the rest of her drink in one action. It was useless to remember and wish, she told herself fiercely. Just remember that he consoled himself pretty damn quick, and on that sage advice she returned to her seat, managing to steer Liz into the row first, with Adam and herself following.

Nat was now three seats away and she prepared to relax and turn her attention to what was going on in front, but afterwards she had very little recollection . . . only her father's performance standing out in her memory.

Gerard Adair, dressed in his Dickensian costume, walked on stage to spontaneous applause and Imogen joined in, proud of her father's popularity. It was difficult for her to be totally objective about him, but no one, she thought, could dispute that he looked an impressive figure, standing out there, alone in the spotlight. He stood for a moment, quite still, waiting for absolute silence, and then he began to speak.

Even his sternest critics acknowledged that Gerard Adair had a voice to envy. It flowed effortlessly across the footlights, rising and falling as he played, with the words, holding the audience in the palms of his hands, his own particular aura filling the huge theatre.

I'll never be as good as he is, thought Imogen a trifle despairingly, and as he took his final bows she listened to the audience reaction with elation. She turned to Adam, her cheeks prettily flushed with pleasure, and heard him say over the noise of the clapping: 'Very good!' and she glowed, for two words of praise from Adam Carlyon were worth half a dozen from anyone else in her eyes. On Adam's far side, Liz leaned forward, clapping heartily, and broke off to give the thumbs-up sign, beaming her approval. Nat Beaumont, she noticed, applauded with less vigour, but at least he had made the effort, and then her conscience smote her. Whatever Nat's personal views were of her father, and it was common knowledge in the theatre world that they 'agreed to differ' on many issues, he was not small-minded enough to begrudge him deserved applause.

For the rest of the programme Imogen found herself remembering how, as a child, she daydreamed of the roles reversed, she receiving the ovation on stage and her father watching her, full of pride and admiration. This particular romance occurred often, and well into her young teens. Over the past few years it had been put away as all childish dreams needed to be, and why she was remembering it now, she had no idea. Unless it was a wishful thought to return to the happy, untroubled days of childhood?

When the final curtain came down, Adam observed:

'No point in trying to move yet, there's always a crush.' He glanced at his wife. 'Elizabeth, as you're dying to have a gossip with Imogen, perhaps we should change places and make it easier for you?' and he raised an amused brow.

Liz stood up with alacrity, commenting teasingly: 'How is it that women gossip and men have intelligent conversations?' and Imogen, seeing the intimate look pass between her two friends as they crossed over, felt a momentary pang of envy. Her eyes touched on Nat, beyond Liz, who was looking at her with chilling deliberation, and Imogen was the first to turn away.

As soon as she was seated, Liz asked: 'You are coming to have a meal with us, Imogen, aren't you?' and her kind, warm interest touched Imogen, as it always did. Elizabeth Carlyon was a cheerful, outgoing young woman in her early thirties. Seven years of marriage and two young children had not managed to dampen the element of the daredevil tomboyishness of her youth. She had met Adam Carlyon while working backstage at the theatre where he was artistic director and after a somewhat turbulent courtship, they had married, surprising some. But Liz's warm, generous personality was a good foil for Adam's quieter but nonetheless strong one, and to Imogen's eyes they seemed the epitome of a truly happy marriage.

Seeing Liz's genuine concern, Imogen replied quickly: 'Yes, please, I'm looking forward to coming, but don't wait on here for me. I must have a quick word with Pa before I leave and then I'll get a taxi.'

Liz looked dubious at that, but did not argue. 'Do say how disappointed we are that he won't be able to join us,' she urged, 'and tell him we thought he was super, as usual!' She eyed the younger girl consideringly. 'Do you wish, now, that you were going with him to America?'

Imogen hesitated briefly and replied: 'I would have liked to have gone, if only to see the place, and it would have been different if he'd been taking the full company, like the South African tour . . .' she pulled a face, '. . . which I missed through being ill.'

'I remember. You had glandular fever, didn't you?'

Imogen nodded. 'Anyway, with a one-man show we thought it would be better if I stayed behind. He's only taking Duggan and a stage manager.' Her eyes went beyond Liz to Adam, deep in conversation with Nat Beaumont, and she went on enthusiastically: 'In any case, I'm looking forward to working with Adam.'

'Your father's loss is our gain,' observed Liz. 'Gerard flies out tomorrow?'

'Yes, poor thing. He hates flying. It is kind of you and Adam to have me stay with you, Lizzie. I know Pa rather forced your hand . . .'

'Nonsense, we'll love having you. What's the point in having guestrooms that are empty? You can stay as long as you like.'

Imogen replied gratefully: 'Thank you, but I shall find somewhere of my own eventually, but I know Pa will go off tomorrow feeling happier knowing I'm staying with friends.' She smiled ruefully. 'He is rather over-protective, I know, and I go along with him for his peace of mind. So I am grateful, especially when you must have your hands full with the children.'

Liz grinned. 'I'm dreadfully spoilt. Adam, bless him, insists I have help in the house, but with Michael at play school for the mornings and Plum being so good that she only wakes for grub and cuddles, life's tremendously organised.'

'When my goddaughter has the beautiful name of Victoria, how can you call her Plum!' protested a laughing Imogen, and Liz shrugged, explaining drolly:

'She arrived, if you remember, at the same time as a bountiful crop of Victoria plums, and somehow fruit and sister became mixed up for Michael, and Plum she's been ever since.' Her attention was distracted by Nat, walking leisurely along the row towards the gangway. She murmured wickedly, 'Now there's a gorgeous hunk of manhood, Imogen. What do you think?'

'He . . . is rather impressive,' Imogen answered.

'Out of all Adam's friends he's one of my favourites. The pity of it is I just can't get him married off! Nat's a self-confessed bachelor, although that was Adam's creed too, once upon a time, and look at him now, poor man. Utterly weighted down by responsibilities!'

'He doesn't look too bad on them,' teased Imogen, watching Adam join Nat and stand talking. They made a startling contrast, both tall, Nat slightly broader across the shoulders, both emanating an inner strength of character, yet Adam, the elder of the two, dark, almost sombre and Nat, fair, tanned and despite his relaxed manner, radiating a vitality that almost sparked.

'I suppose knowing Nat's background it's understandable that he's so disillusioned about marriage,' Liz went on reflectively, and Imogen withdrew her appraisal of the two men and turned her attention to her friend, knitting her brows as she asked:

'What do you mean?'

Liz pulled a face and shrugged. 'Oh, there's a high rate of divorce in his family. He has two sisters with a failed marriage each ... and I don't think his parents got on.'

An actress of some repute had now joined the two men and soon all three were laughing at something she had said.

'Lizzie, do you ever get jealous?'

Liz looked at her friend sharply before following her gaze to the threesome. 'I'd be a liar if I said no,' she replied slowly. 'The theatre's not an easy profession to be in, dealing as it does in dreams and emotions. It's not difficult to forget that the world outside is the real one and people are thrown together in a tight community, depending on each other, sometimes mistaking that for something else. When I married Adam I decided early on that the word I'd cling to was trust. Without trust a marriage is nothing. Adam's thrown up against so many women that if I didn't trust him our whole relationship would be eaten up with jealousy and suspicion. I know a lot of actresses find him attractive and make a play for him. I just have to hope that the children and I mean more to him than a passing fancy ... and if the fancy became more important, then I wouldn't want to hold him.'

There was silence between them and then Imogen commented:

'There are long and lasting marriages in our profession.'

'Of course there are—you just don't hear about them so much.' Liz grinned. 'I'm very fond of Nat, but he always gives me the impression of being so totally in control that I like trying to needle him. Unfortunately he has a formidable mind and such polished manners that I haven't succeeded yet!'

Imogen remained silent. She knew only too well what Liz meant. Adam strolled back along the row and she saw Nat walk up the aisle with the actress, deep in conversation.

'Time to go.' Adam smiled at Imogen. 'Don't let Gerard keep you too long. We shall be expecting you.'

Imogen followed instructions and found the dressing room allocated to her father. She tapped on the door and opened it, and Duggan, folding Gerard's costume prior to packing it away in a case, said encouragingly:

'Sir, here's Miss Imogen!'

The room showed signs of having had a number of occupants, but it was empty of them now. Gerard was seated before the mirror, in the act of knotting his bow tie. Imogen crossed quickly and threw her arms round his neck.

'Darling, you were wonderful—I was so proud! Adam and Liz send their congratulations.' She kissed his forehead. 'How did you feel it went?'

Gerard pursed his lips, but she could tell he was pleased.

'Oh . . . not bad,' and he rose and offered his front to Duggan, who rescued the tie and expertly knotted it. Imogen picked up the clothes brush from the table and waited while Duggan assisted with the evening suit jacket and then she proceeded to give her father a quick brush down.

'Not bad?' she mimicked, winking at Duggan. 'You're always your own sternest critic, Pa.' She eyed her handiwork, flicked the brush once more for good measure and transferred her gaze to the mirror and her father's reflection. 'You were good—take it from your next sternest critic!' and father and daughter smiled at each other. 'You know, Pa, you get more and more handsome every day.' She gave him a quick kiss. 'I must go now.'

Gerard looked at his watch and frowned. 'So must I.'

Imogen moved to the door. 'What time tomorrow, Duggan?'

'I have ordered breakfast for seven o'clock, Miss Imogen.'

'Right. Have a lovely time with the bigwigs, Pa. Give my regards to the Royals,' she added saucily, and blowing them both a kiss she hurried out.

As Imogen collected her jacket from the cloakroom, she reflected, not for the first time, on how lucky they were to have Duggan. She could never remember a time when he was not there and, apart from occasional visits to his sister, was part and parcel of their lives. His loyalty and support were unwavering and although he never slipped from his part of being Gerard's employee, there was a strong bond between the two men and Imogen held him in deep affection.

As she hurried through the theatre Imogen's thoughts now turned to the rest of the evening. She had been silly not to ask Liz if Nat was to be a member of the party going on to The Oasis. She had not asked because she could not make up her mind what she wanted the answer to be. One half of her desperately wanted him to disappear as suddenly as he had appeared, while the other half wanted another chance to show herself, as well as Nat, that his presence affected her not one whit. That both made a mockery of each other she was well aware. She was not allowed to wait long for enlightenment.

It was with a curious sense of detachment that she observed a figure peel itself from a group gathered at the bar and cross with unhurried gait to stand in her path. As his hands gave the jacket she was shrugging herself into the necessary lift into place, time rushed backwards.

Imogen said a cool: 'Thank you,' before opening her clutch bag and taking out a pair of fine leather gloves.

'Very nice.' Nat appraised the fur. 'Is it real?'

Imogen gave him a measured look. 'No, it isn't, as you very well know. I can't afford a real fur, and even if I could, I wouldn't. It's against my principles.' She began to walk, pulling on her gloves, and Nat fell into step.

'*Those* principles I heartily concur . . . but you're not hard up, surely?'

Imogen stopped. 'What do you want, Nat?' She steeled herself to look straight into his eyes, which narrowed at her question.

'Now why should you think I want anything, Imogen?'

She pressed her lips together in frustration, not fooled by the blandness of his expression, and continued on down the stairs.

'Adam merely asked me to wait and bring you along,' he explained, nodding to an acquaintance but not breaking his stride.

'You shouldn't have troubled. I said I'd take a taxi.'

'Oh, it's no trouble. There was someone I had to see, and then I propped up the bar and that too was no hardship. Neither is escorting the beautiful Miss Adair. But you can take a taxi if you wish.'

Imogen took a deep breath. The dry, mocking tone was enough to try the patience of a saint! Stepping down from the last tread, she said with great sweetness:

'That would be rather foolish, wouldn't it, if we're both going to the same place?'

'Extremely foolish.'

'And I've never been beautiful!' The minute it was out Imogen wished it unsaid. If he thought she wanted smarmy compliments she would soon disabuse him!

'We'll not argue,' Nat said smoothly. 'Shall we go? We seem to be attracting some curious looks, hovering, as we are, neither in nor out.'

It was true. They were blocking the doorway.

'The car is parked in a side road,' Nat went on, cupping her elbow with his hand, and Imogen allowed herself to be drawn forward out of the theatre. She was unresisting. There was only so much one could do against the machinations of fate. As they stepped along, side by side, Nat's hand more firmly gripping her arm, guiding, Imogen felt as though the clock had been turned back and the past three years were wiped clean.

CHAPTER TWO

'Now do I frown on thee with all my heart'

THE car turned out to be a Mercedes-Benz, metallic blue in colour and in mint condition, with pale grey leather upholstery and matching carpet.

'Have you sold the Ferrari?' Imogen found herself asking, as she was assisted into the passenger seat, and Nat said: 'No,' before walking round and getting in his side, adding dryly: 'This is one of the perks of my three-year exile,' before starting the engine and extricating the car with precise and minimal effort out of the parking slot and into the main stream of traffic.

Determined to keep things on a general level, Imogen observed conversationally:

'It was a successful evening, don't you think?' The silence that followed was too long for comfort. In the past Nat had never been keen on hiding behind trivialities, and Imogen began to panic. They would have to talk some time, really talk, but she was not ready. Rain spots were beginning to land on the windscreen with increasing regularity and Nat started the wipers before answering with a laconic:

'Artistically or monetarily?'

Imogen breathed an inward sigh of relief. No personal questions for the moment, then. There was to be an unspoken truce. She recalled the question hurriedly and gave a lift to her shoulders.

'I guess I mean artistically, although for the organisers' sakes I'm glad it was a sell-out.'

'The two don't necessarily go together. I suppose it was all right, if you like that sort of thing.'

'But you don't.' Imogen's words were a statement, and he eyed her with deliberation before replying:

'I didn't say that.'

'I beg your pardon. I thought you were implying it.'

Another look, the voice a drawl. 'The whole thing was too predictable. Generally speaking, I found the show boring and artistically chickening out.'

Anger, among other emotions, began to stir. She said coldly:

'I see.'

Amusement tinged his voice. 'Do you?'

Traffic lights changed against him and he was obliged to stop. Imogen watched the windscreen wipers making short shrift of the now heavy rain and wished with all her heart that she could annihilate Nathaniel Beaumont with as much expertise.

'What would *you* have offered the distinguished audience tonight?' she demanded, not able to let the thing drop. 'It's all very easy to sit back and criticise.'

'Isn't it just?' The Mercedes purred forward. 'I can't answer your question off the cuff, but I'd hope for a little more originality. I didn't expect to enjoy tonight. I bought a ticket for the cause, not because I thought I'd be enthralled. I've become disenchanted with these do's over the years. There was the odd highlight . . . the modern ballet was good, I thought.' He paused for a moment and then went on in an enlightened voice:

'Ah! Your protective little claws are out on your father's behalf!'

'Your opinion of him doesn't interest me,' she declared flatly.

'Good, because where Gerard's concerned you can't be objective, and in any case, he's quite capable of standing up for himself.'

Imogen pressed her lips together, clamping her jaw until it ached, and stared out of the window. She was not the only one with claws out, and Nat made a formidable opponent, as she knew to her cost. She huddled lower in the seat. The inside of the car was warm and intimate, giving off an odour of leather and polish and the hint of Nat's aftershave. She turned her head fractionally, taking in the thick fair hair, the good cloth of the evening suit, the long, slender fingers curled round the steering wheel. The Merc was very much in Nat's style, she decided. Sleek, charming to look at, expensive and fast.

Outside The Oasis, Nat leaned across and opened her door, and Imogen involuntarily flattened back against the seat to avoid contact. If he noticed her recoil he did not show it, merely saying:

'Hop out and run. I'll park the car.'

Imogen did as she was told and made a dash for it, fur collar held high for protection from the steady downpour. Once inside she asked for the Carlyon party and was directed to their table. Adam saw her coming and met her, relieving her of her jacket and then escorting her to the table. Not all the guests from the theatre had extended their evening, and a quick glance told Imogen that the redhead was missing. Adam seated Imogen next to himself while Liz, opposite, said with some dismay:

'Oh, dear, didn't Nat find you?'

'Yes, he's gone to park the car,' Imogen told her, and Liz sat back with barely concealed satisfaction. If the whole thing had not been so bizarre, Imogen would have been amused at her friend's matchmaking; as it was, she wished Liz had not been so industrious. She looked round, taking in the soft lights and tasteful decor. A waltz was being played by a trio—piano, bass and drums, and a few diners were dancing.

Imogen saw Nat enter and stand for a moment, his gaze passing unhurriedly round the dining room. He made an impressive figure; the twirling, glittering lights above the dance floor highlighting his fairness; his height automatically causing him to stand out. Spotting their table, he began to wend his way towards them, edging the dance floor, stopping briefly to speak to a couple from the Carlyon party who were dancing.

As he broke away and came nearer, Imogen thought how confident and self-assured he looked, answerable to no one but himself. An aesthete, with charm and good looks and a slightly mocking air, who viewed the world and its inhabitants through wary and cynical eyes. A man capable of writing off a mistake with cool assessment and then getting on with his life in the direction he determined. A loner by intention rather than accident.

She saw more than one woman's head turn as he passed. For someone with his looks and physique he was amazingly unnarcissistic and he was able to ward off any unwanted female advances with an urbanity that was as impenetrable as a brick wall. As he approached their table Adam exclaimed:

'Here's Beau now,' and Nat slid into the seat next to Liz's, rain drops glistening on his hair and shoulders.

'Beau?' Imogen could not help herself, and Adam grinned slyly at his friend across the table.

'Oh, yes ... Beau, indeed! Derived from under-graduate days, wasn't it, Nat? Even then he had a nice way of dressing, and with a name like Beaumont, what could you expect?'

Nat picked up the menu, eyeing Adam over its edge, observing reproachfully:

'I now expect loyalty, and can do without you reminding me. It's a difficult alias to live up to, and I try to keep it quiet.'

Liz grinned. 'It suits you, though, Nat. I've always thought it a pity that you don't act. I can see you perfectly as the Scarlet Pimpernel or Beau Geste . . .'

Nat tilted her a pained glance. 'Lizzie, my dear, your taste leans absurdly towards the romantic.'

'Yes, I know. Adam's given me up. But seriously, Nat, have you never acted?'

'Oh, yes, way back at university.'

'Nat's always been happier at the telling rather than the doing,' put in Adam dryly, and Nat's smile deepened.

The two latecomers gave their order, both waiving the first course, and as Adam poured some wine, he turned to Imogen.

'Was Gerard pleased with the way things went?'

She accepted the glass and shrugged: 'You know Pa, never fully satisfied,' and she sipped the wine appreciatively.

Adam lifted his hands expressively. 'No true artist ever is, my dear. I thought Gerard was on top form tonight and imagine this tour of his will go down well in America. They love Dickens over there.'

'Here's hoping you're right.' Imogen paused and went on tentatively: 'I'm wondering whether to persuade Pa to concentrate just on the acting after next season, Adam.' Steak with side salad was placed before her and as she tucked into her meal she thought about Adam Carlyon and what a good, rock-like friend he was, and how he had come to their aid more than once in the past. He had a slim, angular face and dark compelling eyes set beneath thick, dark brows. He was half French, but was accentless, only the expansive use of his hands betraying his Gallic ancestors. A head of black hair was going attractively grey at the temples, giving a distinguished look to his rather aquiline features.

'How is Gerard, healthwise?' Adam asked. 'Any recurrence of his old trouble?' he added quietly, and Imogen shook her head. 'Fifty-eight isn't old, if one has one's health. Our profession, like everything else, is being hit by the recession and I suppose Gerard has to work harder than perhaps he ought. Money is short and a theatre seat becomes a luxury. I shouldn't worry, Imogen. Gerard's no stranger to the traumas of running his own company and although it's dear to his heart I'm sure he won't hang on to it longer than he feels it's right to do so.'

'I've said the same thing to myself,' admitted Imogen. 'I wonder why everything always sounds so much more sensible when you say it? Thank you, Adam.'

'If it's the business side of things that's beginning to worry you, why don't you have a word with Nat? He's an . . .'

'Oh, that's not necessary,' broke in Imogen hurriedly. She smiled, raising the glass to her lips, thinking wryly that Nat would be the last person to ask, and her eyes were drawn to where he was sitting. Startled, she found herself being studied, a strangely calculating stare. She could not put her finger on the look, but it disturbed her and she broke contact, returning her eyes to her plate, and the next time she looked both chairs were empty and a quick glance showed Liz and Nat preparing to dance. When Adam's attention was next free, she asked casually:

'How long have you known Nat Beaumont, Adam?'

Adam followed the direction of her gaze, smiling lazily at Liz, who grinned impudently across Nat's shoulder before being lost behind other dancers.

'Beau?' Adam twisted slightly in his chair to regard her fully: 'He produced a full text version of *Hamlet* when he was at Oxford and I was invited by somebody, can't remember who . . . I'd been in the business for about eight years and I met Beau afterwards and we struck up a friendship that's lasted ever since. It was obvious then that he had talent, but he was reading law.'

'I didn't know that,' murmured Imogen, crumbling a morsel of bread roll between her fingers as she listened. 'Yet it's not hard to believe. He sounds like a lawyer sometimes—all logic and facts.'

Adam smiled his agreement. 'He practised for a while in the family firm, more to please his father, I believe. Not long after, his father died and he sold up. Came to me, actually, and worked for a spell as my associate, but he diversified into television, did a time in films, then back to the theatre. Bit of a maverick, is Beau. He hasn't lost touch with the law, either. He has a partnership in an advisory business in London.'

Imogen said slowly: 'I've never really understood why Pa and Nat didn't get on. Do you know, Adam?'

'I doubt there's anything specific, more a clash of personalities, activated on Gerard's side, I'm afraid.'

'I know Nat wrote a couple of outspoken articles on theatre policy . . .'

'. . . which Gerard unfortunately took personally,' Adam finished wryly. 'Nat was also on the Arts Council for a time and Gerard was refused a grant . . . he accused Nat of tilting the balance against him. It's a pity. In many respects they're rather alike, although they started out differently. Gerard, as you know, began as an actor and reached quite a high standard before going into directing. Nat has only ever been interested in the manipulating. Both are clever at their job, Gerard has already proved himself and has a strong reputation. Nat's will be made by the two Australian films . . . they're damn good . . . won't be box office successes, but they'll appeal to a critical minority. They're both ready to take risks—how many actor/managers are there about today, like Gerard? Not many. And Beau can give the profession a shot in the arm, which it needs to survive. A very determined young man.'

'Young?' quizzed Imogen, and Adam gave a lopsided smile.

'Young to me, my dear. To an old married man

like me, a bachelor in his thirties is young!'

'You wouldn't go back, Adam,' she accused, 'not to your bachelor days,' and he smiled fully.

'You're right—I wouldn't.'

'And I never think of you as being old! Don't forget I know your birthday, and forty-three isn't old.'

'I'm glad to hear it! Unfortunately it's other people who make me feel my years . . . you, for instance. No bigger than this high when I first saw you, and now look at you!' and their affectionate laughter was broken by Liz and Nat returning from the dance floor, and Liz saying:

'I'm glad you've cheered up. You looked so serious a minute ago that I thought you'd end up weeping in each other's wine!' She sank down into her seat and beamed happily round. 'Thank you, Nat, for that little jig.' Her eyes lit up. 'Ah! Now here is something worth being serious about,' and she turned her attention to the difficult business of choosing from the pudding trolley.

Imogen was conscious of Nat's eyes upon her and wondered uneasily if he was going to ask her to dance, finding herself in an agony of indecision. Should she accept or make an excuse? He did not ask her, so the problem was resolved. It was not a completely wasted evening. Liz and Adam were always good fun and Imogen could see that Nat would be a welcome addition to any dinner party, especially a theatrical one. His ironic observations were wickedly amusing.

When the party began to break up, Imogen went to collect her coat and on returning found to her horror that Liz was busy organising her another lift with Nat. There was nothing either of them could do about it without causing comment, and Nat murmured for her ear alone:

'You can always get out at the end of the street.'

General goodnights were made and then she was walking to the car park with Nat, too tired to argue.

It had stopped raining, but the air was misty and damp. As the Mercedes gained speed, Nat asked crisply: 'I take it you'll put up with my company now we're on the way?' and without giving her a chance to demur, he went on: 'Do you still stay at the same hotel when in London?'

The question was a legitimate one, yet charged the air with provocative memories. Imogen murmured that she did and Nat swung the car in that direction.

'Perhaps one of us should drop the hint to Liz that she's batting on a sticky wicket.' His voice was without inflection.

'As it's highly unlikely we shall be in their company again together, I don't feel it's necessary,' Imogen returned shortly, and for a while there was silence, broken by Nat asking:

'How long have you known them? The Carlyons, I mean.'

At least this line of conversation was safe and they could hardly spend the journey in silence, thought Imogen.

'Liz I met for the first time at their wedding, but I've known Adam—oh, ever since I can remember! When I was young, five, I think, I played the princeling child in *The Caucasian Chalk Circle* and Adam was in it with my father directing.' She paused and added warmly: 'Adam's an old friend.'

'I see.'

The words were flat and Imogen shot him a glance, but his face told her nothing. He said:

'I understand Gerard is off to America tomorrow.

How brave of him to leave you behind.' There was a hard, granite core to the bantering tone. 'And what are you going to be doing while he's away?'

It was bound to happen. It had been a mistake to remind him that their meeting tonight was accidental and not likely to be repeated, and he was past master at the art of verbal attack. She replied defensively:

'I'm joining the company at Queensbridge.' There was a silence which she felt compelled to break. 'I'm playing Rosalind in *As You Like It*. I've never worked for Adam before and I'm looking forward to it enormously. I've a great respect for Adam.'

'The devil you have!'

Imogen turned her head in surprise to find Nat's face wore a decidedly sardonic expression.

'Just what is that supposed to mean?' she demanded. 'Don't you agree that Adam is talented?'

'I agree entirely.'

'Then why the sneer?'

Nat swung into a side street and the hotel came into view. There was a convenient parking space not far from the entrance and he pulled into it, switching off the engine and dowsing the lights before turning to eye her with chilling deliberation.

'Was it a sneer? I think you're being unduly sensitive.' He pushed open the door and slid out, crossing in front to come round to her side, and a solitary street light showed his face to be smoothed out into a blank mask. In seething silence Imogen removed herself with as much speed as her slim-fitting dress and temper allowed, muttered a controlled: 'Thank you for the lift,' and without looking at him began to walk briskly towards the hotel entrance, head erect, the high heels of her evening shoes making sharp, metallic tapping noises as she moved quickly across the pavement. The minute she realised that he had joined her she stopped.

'Just what are you doing?' The peremptory question was made more eloquent by the haughty lift of her finely shaped brows and the speaking look from the bristling grey eyes. Nat put a hand beneath her bent arm and scooped her along for a few more steps, saying:

'I'm seeing you to your room.'

She shrugged him off and again stopped in her tracks.

'It isn't necessary.' Icicles could not have been colder.

'Nevertheless, I'm doing so.' The tone was mildness itself. 'It's too late for you to be wandering round on your own. Gerard wouldn't like it, and neither do I.' His mouth twisted. 'For once we would be in total agreement.'

Imogen gave him a wintry smile. 'He'll be delighted to know.'

'I doubt it, and you'll be a fool to tell him I'm back. You'll not get him on that plane tomorrow, if you do.'

Without a word Imogen swung on her heel and stalked towards the hotel, through the lobby, and collected her key with the briefest of greetings to the night clerk, and in continuing silence they entered the lift.

Once outside her room Imogen said with studied patience:

'Now you've seen me home, you can go.' And to hell with you, hung on the air.

'Home?' Nat passed a critical eye round the empty corridor, looking the picture of ease and in no way put out by her hostility. He assessed the stereotype doors leading off at intervals, the bare paint-washed walls, the slightly shabby carpet.

She turned the key savagely in the lock. 'You know what I mean,' she threw over her shoulder, unsure of him, and of herself, and worn out emotionally. Her one idea was to escape this disturbing individual who had walked back into her life so unexpectedly and gain the sanctuary of her room.

'Have you ever had a real home, Imogen?'

The question threw her off balance and she lifted her head, eyes wary and alert. He now leaned one shoulder against the wall as he gazed down at her, brows raised enquiringly. There appeared to be nothing of any significance in the question, but she could not trust him to be anything but devious and attack was her only weapon.

'I thought I had one, once,' she returned stonily, 'but it was built of straw.' She swung away. 'And home can be anywhere. Goodnight.' And goodbye! she added fiercely to herself.

Nat caught her by the arm. 'Aren't you going to invite me in, Imogen?'

'No, I'm not.'

'Dear me, that's not a very wifely act.' He paused. 'Is it, Mrs Beaumont?'

'Don't call me that,' Imogen said icily, and as he affected puzzlement, she repeated impatiently: 'Don't call me Mrs Beaumont!'

'Forgive me, but I was under the impression that that was your name? Imogen Beaumont.' He drawled the name. 'But perhaps you've done something about changing it, of which I'm unaware?'

'You know damn well I haven't!'

'Why?' The question was careless, and when she looked blank he asked it again with almost gentle patience. 'Why haven't you changed it?'

She floundered: 'Well . . . you . . . I thought you'd do something.' Her eyes flashed. 'It was you who said our marriage wouldn't work!'

'You agreed, if I remember correctly, but that's an old story. So why are you still Imogen Beaumont?'

'Now is hardly the time . . .'

'You suggest we meet tomorrow? Perhaps Gerard would like to join us?'

'. . . nor the place . . .'

'I did hint that you might invite me in. There are things to be discussed.'

'Yes, I know. But not now. It's too late.' There was a tiny thread of desperation in her voice and Imogen heard it and was mortified. Keep cool, she thought frantically.

'You can surely tell me why you're still Imogen Beaumont.' Nat was all mild persuasion.

'I . . . I call myself Adair.'

'So I gather, but legally you're still Beaumont. My monthly cheque still goes into the account of Mrs Imogen Beaumont . . .'

'I don't touch a penny of it! I wish you'd stop sending it . . . I don't want your money . . .'

'. . . and I'm surprised that Gerard didn't insist on the lawyers being brought in. Ah! I can see that he tried. Why didn't you let him have his way and wipe the slate clean, Imogen? Hardly anyone knew, it would have been quite easy.'

'Because I wanted to forget! and I thought you'd do something about it. Why didn't you do something?'

'Because it suits me to be married.'

For a moment she stared uncomprehendingly and then realisation dawned and she said scornfully: 'Of course—what a let-out! All the fun and a cast-iron excuse!'

'Quite so. After years of good sense and logical thinking I allowed myself to behave irrationally. I made the mistake of thinking we'd be different. Well, we weren't. I always knew I wasn't made for nuptial bliss and I'm not. I believe I've apologised for this fault, have I not? I've no intention of making the same mistake again, so having a wife in the background suits me. When it ceases to suit you, you'll have to let me know. Perhaps there's already someone eager to make you change your name again? . . . or do the young men find it difficult to get past Daddy's eagle eye?' He grinned with sardonic amusement. 'Do you think Gerard would mind if I claimed the kiss I didn't get when I left for the Antipodes?' and the green eyes mocked, enjoying the heightened colour in her cheeks and the sparkling eyes as she glared back at him.

'I'm sure there was someone else more than ready to take my place!' she retorted contemptuously, and then his hands swung her to him as he said, velvet-smooth:

'Oh, there was, my dear, there was . . . but I still claim what was mine.'

Though her senses were outraged, there was a sharp, bitter-sweet feeling of recognition—a coming home, as her body was curved and moulded to his by the insistence of his hands.

The kiss was insultingly intimate, his body flaunting the knowledge that they had shared such an embrace many times before, the memories leaping through her, shrieking out a denial of any response on her part. Imogen suffered the indignity of that kiss, knowing it was useless to resist, for Nat had more strength in one hand then she had totally, pride whipping up the anger she needed to save face.

When the pressure of his mouth lifted, she drew breath for a biting speech, but the words were blocked again before making form.

This time the kiss was soft and treacherously seductive, his hands gentled, beckoning a response from her emotionally starved body. She quivered and trembled as his lips brushed eyelids and cheek, returning to her tremulous lips. The heat raced through her and she was aware of the exquisite melting of flesh and bones and the spiral of joy beginning a slow growth, deep inside her.

And then she was free and she could breathe and needed the wall for support. With the withdrawal she found herself stripped of all her defences, and panic struck her. She had learned for three years to forget how it felt to be in his arms and in a pityingly few seconds her body had surrendered to the memory. Her mind and reason came out of paralysis and her hand came up in a wide arch and struck him a blow across the chin, followed by a low and impassioned:

'I hate you, Nat Beaumont! Why can't you just go away and stay out of my life!'

Seemingly in no way put out by her attack, Nat drawled:

'That might be easier said than done,' catching her wrists before she could do any more harm, holding her in a restricting grasp until he felt the tension leave her body. For a few seconds he stood without moving. Imogen's forehead rested on his shirt front. His jacket was open, falling either side, enveloping her, and she could feel the strong, rapid pounding of his heart, matching her own, beat for beat.

'Have you finished fighting?' he murmured, and she gave a resigned movement of the head. He released his grip and splayed his hands, palm downwards, on the wall either side of her head, in no hurry to move.

In a low voice, Imogen said: 'Let me go.' The heat from his body fused with her own, making a leaping assault on her senses.

'Please, Nat,' he chided softly.

The tip of her tongue moistened her lower lip, leaving it wet and glistening. She swallowed hard, and then said:

'Please . . . Nat.'

A second's pause and his weight lifted, the thrust coming from his palms, his long length peeling away in a sweeping movement from chest to loins.

Imogen set her lips stubbornly, lifting her eyes to his face, wiping her own free of expression. She was damned if she was going to give him the satisfaction of seeing what a shattering effect he had had on her.

With rather an enigmatic smile, Nat remarked: 'It seems I'll have to show you how to really pull a punch.' He took her unresisting right hand and folded the fingers into a fist. 'That's far more effective,' he added, and he brought it gently into contact with his jaw, keeping it there for a few seconds. Then he said: 'Goodnight, Imogen. It's good to be home,' and carefully giving back her hand, he turned her round, pushed wide the door, and firmly propelled her through.

Imogen heard the door click shut. She walked to the bed and threw herself face downwards. She could still feel the impression of his body against hers and a poignant ache seared through the pit of her stomach, and she raised a fist and drove it violently down into the soft depths of the pillow, crying: 'Damn him! Damn him! Damn him!'

The cat, who had been happily curled up, fast asleep at the bottom of the bed, and had opened an indignant eye when she had first thrown herself down, now sprang off in fright and took refuge underneath.

Her burst of anger spent, Imogen dragged herself up and with rigid singlemindedness made ready for sleeping. After a while the cat slunk out from under the bed and sat watching her, amber eyes unwinking.

As she sat before the dressing table, pyjama-clad, wiping the remains of make-up from her face, Imogen paused and studied her reflection, tilting her head first one way and then the other, her eyes seeking something, she did not know what, to reassure her.

'I look just the same now as I did before I left this room earlier,' Imogen said out loud, 'but I'm not, Poss.'

The cat twitched an ear.

'It's good to be home.' The sound of his voice mocked her. She could see, in her mind's eye, a farmhouse, built of Norfolk stone, sheltered from the east coast winds by a line of sycamores, pale pinky-mauve clematis climbing round the front door and bright red poppies dancing in the breeze. The house seemed to be smiling in the sunshine and an Irish setter was lying across the stone step, asleep.

'Where thou art—that—is home!'

Imogen frowned. The fragment of a poem was teasing her subconscious . . . one line persisting . . . an Emily Dickinson . . . 'where thou art—that—is home!'

With pensive face she opened the lid of a small round box placed in the centre of the dressing-table. Inside was an assortment of jewellery and using the tip of a finger she sifted and probed until a small space was uncovered.

For a long while Imogen gazed at the twinkling gold band, before tilting it on to its narrow edge, so that it encircled the end of her finger, its position precarious.

Precarious. That was exactly the right word. A precarious balance—exactly how we were, she thought sadly. Casually she sloped her finger and the ring stood for a second on its end, unsupported, and then circled round once to drop back on to the dark velvet base of the box.

Imogen closed the lid with a sudden snap and raised her eyes, not seeing her own face, but rather a series of images ... Nat, looking down at her from the top of the sand dune, Nat laughing as she tried to secure the sail on the *Pandora*, Nat as he had slipped the wedding ring on to her finger ... like a camera, all frozen shots of Nathaniel Beaumont ... her husband.

Imogen turned abruptly from the mirror and went to bed.

The next morning she was awake before the alarm and remembered that Nat was back in England. Even in the unlikely event that she had forgotten, her bruised lip would have reminded her.

Throwing back the covers, she crossed to the mirror and touched it tenderly with the tip of her tongue. The cat leaped up on to the dressing-table and watched her, and she frowned down at him and said soberly:

'Well, Poss, old boy, he's back in our lives, and you'll be pleased to know that I made a bodge of the whole thing.' On that expansive note she swept into the bathroom. While she showered and dressed she tangled with the problem, not able to leave it alone. One thing was certain, she should never have allowed him to bring her home.

Home! That word again.

She slid a slender leg into a stocking, repeated the action, and then pushed her feet into smart leather shoes, asking herself crossly: Why did I?

Poss yawned. It looked rather like a laugh and Imogen glared at him, saying waspishly:

'Because I wanted to prove that whatever we had shared together three damn years ago was a thing of the past—dead as yesterday's news! All I succeeded in doing was losing my temper.' She began flinging her clothes into her suitcase. 'And it was all rather humiliating.' The Oriental dress was thrown in with force. 'Okay, so memories and intentions have a way of becoming tangled up . . . and don't get me wrong, Poss, there's no longer any love left in me for Nat. He killed that off effectively and swiftly enough the minute I found that girl in his flat. He soon consoled himself, didn't he? and had the gall to admit it, too!' She banged the lid shut, but it would not meet, so she leaned on it. 'Seeing him again brought it all back and threw me off balance, which is quite understandable.' The last words were punctuated by panting as she exerted her strength on the case, and when the catches locked together she straightened up with satisfaction. 'Well, that's that, Poss.' She looked keenly round the room, checking that nothing had been missed. 'I sometimes feel like a snail, moving round with his house on his back, though in my case, it's a case.' She smiled at the play on words and began to apply a light make-up. When she came to her lips she hesitated, lipstick poised.

Why had Nat kissed her like that? His manner the whole evening had been sardonic and mocking, except at the end, right at the end, when he had seemed almost sad. She carefully applied a pretty shade of pink to her lips, a slight frown on her forehead. Had he too been beset by memories? More likely he wanted to remind her of what she was missing! What did it matter? she asked herself impatiently, as she threw the cosmetics into her bag. There was little likelihood of them meeting again— other than in a lawyer's office, so what was she worrying about?

This last inner question ended on a note of exasperation. She checked that the cream blouse and the skirt of her suit fitted satisfactorily, picked up the jacket and her bag and said sternly to Poss:

'You wait here until I get back . . . you can have your breakfast then . . . and no taking a swim in the bath while I'm gone!'

Poss turned his back disdainfully and began his ablutions.

Gerard was already seated at the breakfast table when she walked into the dining room. He looked up at her arrival, a half-read letter in his hand. Imogen kissed him, draped the jacket round the back of her chair and sat down.

'Morning, Pa,' she said cheerfully, unfolding her napkin.

'Good morning, Imogen.' Gerard returned to his letter while breakfast was served and then commented mildly: 'You're looking bright for someone who was out late last night. Did you enjoy yourself?'

Imogen, busy tackling half a grapefruit, wondered what he would say if she replied: Oh, I had a wonderful time. My long-lost husband turned up out of the blue, made my evening hell and kissed me to show that he still had the power to make me want him.

She said instead: 'A lovely time, Pa. The food was delicious and Liz and Adam were great fun. How was your do?'

'Interesting. I pandered to my years and didn't

stay till the end.' Gerard accepted another cup of
tea, asking casually: 'Who was there, apart from the
Carlyons? Anyone I know?'

Imogen gazed at him fondly, firmly shutting out a
blond head and green eyes. 'Darling, you might not
have known all the guests, but they all knew you.
Your praises were sung continuously,' and she
launched into a lighthearted conversation and
amusing anecdotes, finishing with: 'Anything interesting in the post?'

Gerard glanced briefly at the letters by his plate.

'Only a missive from the bank and confirmation
of Norwich for September.'

'Oh, good, we've always been happy there,
haven't we?' and yet she felt uneasy. Norwich was
too near Nat's patch for comfort, and then she dis-
pelled her fears angrily.

She was getting paranoid about that man!

The drive to Heathrow was without incident.
Imogen loved airports and flying, Gerard hated
both. Duggan disappeared to sort out the luggage
and tickets, and Imogen bought three newspapers
and took her father's mind off aeroplanes by finding
the critics' reviews of the gala performance. She
scanned them quickly, pleased that Gerard received
a special praising mention in all three, noting with
less pleasure that two out of the three agreed with
Nat's opinion, voiced the previous evening, that the
show was 'safe'. She read out the pertinent passages
and then folded the papers and tucked them under
Gerard's arm, saying teasingly:

'There, you can read the rest at your leisure, they
should help cover a few thousand miles.'

Gerard smiled dutifully and said suddenly: 'I wish
you were coming with me, Imogen.'

Startled, Imogen replied: 'But, Pa, it's all

arranged. I can hardly let Adam down now, at this late stage,' guilt springing up because she knew she didn't want to. She looked at him anxiously.

'Yes, I know. I wish you were coming, that's all.' Gerard searched her face. 'I've just realised how much I'm going to miss you.'

Imogen rested her head on his shoulder, her arms round his waist.

'You are an old silly! If I wasn't so certain that it was pre-flight nerves I'd come with you right now.' She raised a troubled face. 'Pa, you agreed that it would be better for me to stay behind.'

He patted her shoulder. 'I know, I know.'

'Nothing's changed.' It was half statement, half question.

'No, nothing's changed.' He squeezed her hand, saying brightly: 'We have an exciting programme to tackle in the autumn.'

Imogen nodded. 'Pa, you're not worrying about me, are you? I mean, I am old enough to . . . take care of myself.' She stumbled over this admission, remembering the last time he had gone away and left her, and her issuing the very same reassurances. She hurried on, 'There's lots of girls my age who can't even get a job. You're leaving me very secure with Adam, you know.'

'Yes, yes . . . and it will do you good to work with him.'

'It will be interesting,' conceded Imogen. 'You'll be sure to make the last night of the play?—because I want you out there, in the audience, proudly cheering me on.'

He smiled. 'Yes, I'll be out there—barring fog and hurricanes.'

Imogen said darkly: 'You see you are, or there'll be trouble.'

Duggan loomed up, and their flight was called. Gerard, not a demonstrative man, drew Imogen to him and kissed her briefly, and Imogen hugged him hard, muttering: 'Take care, Pa . . . I'll write.'

A photographer appeared out of nowhere and took their photograph. Gerard was patiently charming, Imogen resigned. She always came out looking like Dracula's mother, but she smiled, making an effort.

While the photographer was getting the details from Gerard, Duggan whispered:

'I'll take care of Sir, Miss Imogen, don't you worry . . . and I'll write to you; let you know how he is.'

Imogen smiled her thanks and gave him a hug and then they were at the barrier. Gerard turned, raised a hand in farewell and went through out of sight.

Imogen leaned against the observation window, idly watching planes taking off and landing. When the British Airways Boeing 747 taxied away from the airport building her attention quickened. The jumbo jet turned its nose towards the main runway, gathering speed, and was up in the air, a grey streak, soon only a pinpoint in the clouds. Before it disappeared completely, Imogen was walking away.

CHAPTER THREE

'What think you of falling in love?'

IMOGEN directed the Rover towards Queensbridge, her thoughts divided between her father, on his way to America, and the exciting weeks that lay ahead of her. She felt a certain amount of relief now that he was actually on his way. Getting Gerard Adair organised on any journey was a mammoth task, even with Duggan's help, and this one had seemed particularly so.

Around midday she felt hunger pangs and pulled off the road into the car park of a small, picturesque hotel. Leaving Poss lying along the back window ledge looking rather like a huge orange cushion, she went in search of food.

The dining room was not busy, Monday was perhaps a light day for travellers, and she found she was the only woman there on her own, but that did not bother her. As she was shown to a table by the window, Imogen was aware of some flattering interest from one or two of the male eyes as she passed the other tables, which pleased her. The sea-green suit was not new, but was a favourite, and its plain lines showed her figure to good advantage. She had always tended to take care of her clothes, choosing classic styles that did not date. Rather bleakly she remembered who had chosen the suit and she took a perverse pleasure in the fact that something Nat had paid for was making her attractive to other men ... there seemed poetic justice in it, somehow.

She ate, and enjoyed her meal, and afterwards, waiting for the arrival of coffee, sat and gazed out of the window. The view was a very English one, pastoral and charming. Gentle, undulating pastures dotted with cows, hedges and patches of woodland, all topped by a pale blue-grey sky. A soothing picture, she thought contentedly. Nat's remark the evening before, about not realising how much he had missed England until he had returned, came to mind.

She frowned. Blast the man!—he was back in her thoughts again, and then she gave an exasperated

sigh. Surely it was time she could think about Nat
without getting neurotic about him . . . time she
exorcised that part of her life once and for all?

Imogen accepted the suggestion that she might
like to sit in the sun-lounge to drink her coffee, and
followed the waiter, settling herself in a comfortable
armchair in a secluded corner. She smiled her thanks
as the coffee was poured and, left alone, contemplated the change of scene. From this window she
could see a giant monkey-tree rising from the centre
of a beautifully kept lawn. It was funny, she had
never liked them, they seemed too artificial somehow.

There had been a monkey-tree, one as large as
that, in the grounds of the convalescent home, she
remembered, sipping her coffee. There had been
squirrels in the surrounding trees too. As she had sat
for the long periods necessary for her recovery, it
had amused her watching their antics.

Perhaps it was time Caffrey's and Nathaniel
Beaumont were exorcised, she decided, her mind
going back and sifting the memories . . .

It was when they were playing the Theatre Royal,
Norwich, that Imogen had gone down with a particularly nasty attack of glandular fever, requiring a
brief but memorable spell in the city hospital. At
first she had been too ill to worry about anything
other than being able to breathe, only the calm,
matter-of-fact manner of the nurses and doctors per-
suading her that she was not at death's door.
Gradually, tiny progress was made, and she then
began to worry about the South African tour that
the Adair Company was about to make.

She was transferred to a convalescent home outside Norwich where, as her strength improved, she
could take gentle walks in the beautiful grounds. At

first, when Gerard visited, by tacit agreement they ignored the tour, but when she began to feel more like her old self she delivered the conclusions of some serious thinking to him, calmly and firmly, as they sat on one of the seats provided in the grounds.

'They say I'll be here for another five days or so,' she told him, 'and then I thought I'd go and stay with the Hunts at Babingley. When they moved last year they invited us over any time, remember? I've already rung to check and it's all right. They sent their best wishes, by the way.' She glanced sideways at him, noting the truculent expression, the deep frown, the jutting lip. 'It's too bad, of course,' she went on lightly. 'I've been looking forward so much to South Africa, but there's nothing we can do about it, is there, Pa?' She waited a moment for an answer and gave him a gentle nudge with her elbow. Gerard looked up and smiled reluctantly.

'No, there's nothing we can do.'

And that was that.

The Hunts were a hardworking couple, in their early forties, childless, who were making a living running a market garden in the area called the Marshlands, to the west of the Great Ouse river. The area's rich soil was good for fruit, crops and flowers, and although some might find the flatness and the lack of hedges or walls uninteresting, for the land was divided by dykes, Imogen had grown to love it.

She also loved the Norfolk burr and often sought conversations with the locals just to hear it. It was early June and that summer was promising to be warm. She had a pleasant and easy relationship with the Hunts—Mary and Colin—could come and go when she pleased and was treated as a daughter of the house. The curious lethargy her illness had left her with was lifting as each day passed. For the first few days she just sat about in the sunshine, reading or resting, Poss curled up on her lap, but gradually her explorations went a little further, and further still. She helped Colin in the fields and greenhouses, enjoying this glimpse into nature's growth and finding a curious satisfaction and peacefulness in the countryside.

The first time she met Nathaniel Beaumont he mistook her for a boy. He had wandered down to the greenhouses in search of Colin Hunt and saw a slim, youthful figure with short-cropped hair, dressed in a check shirt and jeans, wielding a hose, the spray watering a row of young lettuce.

'Hey, lad! Is Colin about?'

Quite naturally, Imogen did not respond at once, curiosity eventually making her turn round. Even then, at this first sight of him, she was immediately attracted. He was dressed in light-coloured pants and an open-necked shirt and she saw that his eyes were an unusual light green. When he took a good look at her he put up his hands, his face showing comic despair.

'I'm so sorry . . . I thought you were . . .'

'A boy? I shall grow my hair instantly,' she replied, her hand going selfconsciously to her hair, the fingers running through the short wavy mop making her look even more of an urchin.

'No, no . . . now that I can see you fully, you are undoubtedly female.' He had an exceedingly pleasing voice, which was now grave, but his eyes were amused and Imogen felt the first stirrings of confusion beneath his gaze.

She grinned, to hide it, quipping: 'I'm very glad to hear it. You're looking for Colin? I'm sorry, he was here a minute ago, but he seems to have disappeared,' and she swung round, glad to have an excuse to break the look, her eyes searching the empty fields. She turned back to him. 'I wonder— perhaps I can help?'

'I rang through with an order about an hour ago. Beaumont's the name . . . Nathaniel Beaumont.'

'In that case, Mr Beaumont, I *can* help.' Imogen turned off the tap, wiping damp hands down the sides of her jeans, before leading the way back towards the house, feeling a tingling all the length of her spine. Suddenly her own body movement, a thing she never normally thought about, thrust itself upon her awareness, due entirely to this man following her. The fact disturbed and annoyed her, so that when they gained the enclosure of the shed where she knew Mary put the orders for collection, her voice was rather offhand as she announced:

'Here it is. Beaumont, Caffrey's Farm. Is that you?' In the cool shade Imogen felt hot and sticky. Her companion, on the other hand, appeared to be untouched by the heat. Cool and implacable was Mr Beaumont. She handed over the box of fruit and vegetables, saying in a businesslike manner:

'What do you do about payment?'

He smiled, and Imogen decided that no man should have so many aces.

'We have an account.' He stood on one side and Imogen walked out, squinting her eyes against the harsh glare of the sun. A young Irish setter was sitting in the back of a bright red Ferrari. On seeing them she stood up, her long pink tongue slavering and her magnificent red plume waving madly.

Nat Beaumont said: 'You can stroke her—she's friendly, too friendly sometimes,' as he placed the box in the car.

Imogen moved forward and touched the silky

head, receiving a wet caress on her arm and another, more generous one on her face. Laughing, she backed off a pace.

'She's lovely. What's her name?'

'Tallulah. Lulu for short.' He waited, smiling slightly. 'If I'm to make a proper introduction I need further information.'

'Imogen,' she supplied obligingly.

'Lulu, meet Imogen . . . Imogen, Tallulah.'

'She's beautiful,' enthused Imogen, stroking the bitch again. 'I shall be in Poss's bad books for this treachery.' Her eyes glanced swiftly round. 'In fact, I'm surprised he hasn't appeared to voice his displeasure.'

'You have a dog?'

'No, a cat—a huge marmalade with an extremely strong character. He's skulking about somewhere.'

'Poss?'

'Short for Poseidon. He loves water and can swim like a fish.'

Nat Beaumont smiled at this piece of information. 'He must be unusual. Poseidon, the sea god—most apt. I trust he's not so enamoured of earthquakes?'

Imogen hid her surprise. It was not everyone who knew that Poseidon was also the god of earthquakes. She grinned. 'I hope not.' She gave the setter a final pat and backed away. 'Well, I'd better get on with the job.'

'Thank you for your help.'

'Not at all.' She turned and walked back towards the fields, rather amused at herself. She had not reached the age of twenty-two without knowing when a man was interested in her, and she wished she had not been so much at a disadvantage, dressed in her working clothes . . . he had even mistaken her for a boy! That paragon did not look as though he would ever be at a disadvantage. Very sure of himself, was Mr Beaumont. And with every justification, a tiny voice whispered slyly inside her head.

She idly watched the gleaming red Ferrari as it wended its way down the track to the main road, some distance away, and when it turned left towards King's Lynn she started the hose going again. Poss stalked majestically along the grass path, his tail waving threateningly. He sat haughtily in the shade of a nearby giant rhubarb bush and stared balefully.

Imogen gently edged the spray nearer. Poss lifted his head and his amber eyes glared. She laughed.

'I thought you might like to cool down,' she teased. 'You can relax, Poss. I liked Lulu, but I liked her master more. Did you see him? A real dish. Tall, good-looking—and that voice! Pure velvet, Poss.'

Poseidon, at that time, was five, and had been Imogen's confidant ever since, as a tiny kitten, she had rescued him from a watery grave. Instead of putting him off water his near-drowning had done the reverse. He now followed her back to the house where Imogen saw the figure of Mary Hunt through the kitchen window.

'Mary, a Mr Beaumont called a while back. I gave him his box of goodies, I hope that was all right?' and she leaned on the window ledge to hear Mary's reply.

'Goodness, yes. Mr Beaumont happens to be our landlord!'

'Oh.' Imogen stared at her blankly. 'Does he live far away?'

'No, you can see the house from our front, just. Caffrey's Farm it's called, though it's not been a farm for a few years now. Mrs Beaumont's folk were Caffreys—been in Norfolk for some generations, I believe. A real old family are the Caffreys.'

Imogen made her way up the stairs, Poss stalking ahead into her bedroom, and she glared at him. 'You can take that satisfied look off your face,' she told him crossly, peeling off her clothes. 'It was a hundred to one chance he'd be married, but if I were his wife I shouldn't be too happy about his way of introducing Lulu to strange females—even if they don't look like one!' She stared at herself in some dismay as she passed the mirror. She had a mud streak across her forehead and the sun had caught her face, which glowed rather alarmingly. She shrugged, thinking, oh well, what does it matter? and went to shower.

Later on in the week Imogen took a bus ride along the coast road, dropping off at the Royal estates of Sandringham, and spent a pleasant couple of hours wandering round the grounds, finishing up with an interesting look at Sandringham Church. The estate was beautifully kept, with controlled picnic areas, the whole enhanced by trees and rhododendrons set back behind wide grass verges. The wrought iron gates added a stately touch to the Victorian Tudor style of the house, which Imogen considered to be unpretentious for a Royal private house and looked more like a happy home, albeit a large one.

Her next port of call was to be the seashore and by a stroke of luck she caught a bus that was going in that direction, trundling down the winding lanes towards the coast. She asked about the times coming back and alighted at the village of Snettisham and then made tracks for the sea. It was farther than she thought. A couple of miles would not bother her usually, but she was not yet back on form after her illness and she arrived puffing and panting at the top of the sand dunes and was glad to flop down into a hollow, topped by coarse marram grass, to catch her breath.

The east coast air was always bracing, but the day was so warm that the breeze from the sea was welcome. Imogen stripped off the top of her sundress with relief and after applying a liberal helping of sun oil to her exposed flesh, she unwrapped her lunch, packed by Mary. As she hungrily took a bite of ham sandwich, her eyes savoured the wide expanse of grey sea in front, wondering just whereabouts in the Wash King Canute was supposed to have tried to stop the incoming tide. She smiled at the thought. Poor man! The long, seemingly endless stretch of beach was deserted her end and Imogen hugged her knees, enjoying her solitary state, feeling an unusual empathy with her surroundings.

Her aloneness was not to remain. She was suddenly interrupted out of her reverie by a shower of sand hurtling across her bare back and a pink tongue licking her face. After the initial shock she held off her friendly assailant as best she could, laughingly protesting:

'Lulu! Hello, girlie . . . no, I don't want a wash, thank you. Yes, I know you're a beauty, but there's no need to . . .'

'Tallulah!'

The stern bellow reached the setter and she lifted her head, ears pricked, tail pointed. She gave Imogen one more wet lick and then bounded off out of sight, up the side of the dune, scattering sand once more as she went. Laughing still, Imogen stood and began to brush the sand from her shoulders, shaking her hair forward with the same intent. A shadow crossed her vision and she turned to look up at the tall, fair-haired figure standing on the edge of the dune, a chastened Lulu by his side.

Really, it is too much, thought Imogen crossly, the way this man always catches me at my worst!

She reasoned instantly that although Nathaniel Beaumont might attract her more than any man before, it did not matter what she looked like, as she had no intention of becoming interested in another woman's husband.

'I'm sorry, has she done any harm?' His voice was short with annoyance and Lulu sank to her belly and gazed up at him with mournful brown eyes, only the tip of her tail giving an anxious twitch.

'No, of course not, I'm flattered by the reception,' Imogen assured him. 'She seems to think I'm her long-lost friend.' She thought he had no business to look so damned attractive! He was wearing a light blue Italian cotton-knit shirt and hip-hugging Levis. His bare feet were pushed into leather-thonged sandals and a broad belt, fastened by an embossed metal buckle, emphasised a slim waist. As he stood, hands on hips, looking down at her, she could see the fair hair shining on his arms, which were nicely tanned, and that the shirt was stretched across a generous spread of chest and shoulder muscle. His hair was damp, showing a tendency to wave and curl at the neck edges, and he carried a wet towel, obviously returning from a swim.

All this was impressed upon her in a sweeping and intent upward glance which she allowed to fall on the abject Lulu as soon as she realised the pleasure she felt just by looking at him.

A cat can look at a king, she told herself stubbornly, resisting the temptation to smooth down her hair in an attempt to repair Lulu's generous greeting. She sank to her knees in the sand and held out a hand, and Lulu padded forward to be gently fondled, the plumed tail beginning to wag more hopefully, brushing the sand in all directions as she lay on her belly.

'I hope you didn't smack her,' Imogen asked anxiously, adding: 'She's not very old, is she?'

The green eyes smiled and amusement tinged his voice. 'I don't have to use brute force on my women as a rule. A stern voice usually does the trick.' His lips twitched.

'I'm sure it does,' Imogen remarked dryly, and suppressed the desire to giggle. He really was outrageous.

The half-smile widened, wickedly, but he merely said: 'She's a youngster still, but she needs to learn her manners. An unruly dog is as bad as a spoilt child, they end up with no one liking them. Down, Lulu!' This last was ordered because the setter, hearing the softening of his voice, had again risen on her haunches, making a wild lunge with the over-free tongue. On the command she sank back, giving another mournful look up at her master.

It was too much, Imogen's giggles broke out into laughter and she stood upright, her eyes brimming.

'Oh, dear—I now know the meaning of the phrase hangdog! One look at those eyes and that expression and I'd be done for!'

It seemed that he was to be endowed with all the envied attributes. The lift of one eyebrow was an accomplishment indeed! And those eyes! Really, what was a girl to do? Escape, and fast, she thought grimly, for at the moment the green eyes were holding much too much open interest for comfort. She became conscious that her sundress was exactly that, one designed for the sun, and its style necessitated being bra-less. The halter neck was perfectly respectable, but this man brought out in her an excessive sensitiveness in her own body which shattered her composure.

Escape or dismissal, both would do. She was just

about to say something conventional and return to
her former position on the sand, when his voice said
sharply:

'Is that your lunch lying there covered in sand?'

Imogen followed his look and shrugged. 'Yes, but
not to worry. I'm not particularly hungry,' and she
hoped that Lulu appreciated her lie. There was
silence for a moment and he said with a drawl to the
words:

'That's rather a pity. The least Lulu and I can do
is to offer you another lunch. We were just going to
find our own.'

Imogen squinted up at him, finding her heart
sinking to her boots. Ah well, it was, perhaps, for the
best. He had sent himself zooming down in her esti-
mation and that was that. She would not even be
able to daydream about him now.

She said in a level voice: 'But perhaps Mrs
Beaumont wouldn't like that.' It was a statement,
not a question. Her grey eyes outstared those amaz-
ing green ones. The only sounds were the waves
breaking regularly against the shore and the bitch's
panting. His face went curiously blank and then
amusement filled his eyes, although his voice was
steady enough.

'Well now . . . I really don't know. We could find
out, I dare say,' he remarked contemplatively. 'A
phone call to New Zealand is nothing, these days.'
One brow quirked. 'But, you know, I doubt the
necessity of asking her. My mother would surely
appreciate the need to compensate you for your lost
lunch, especially if she knew that the owner had a
speaking pair of grey eyes and a lovely pair of
dimples,' and he smiled a slow, lazy smile.

Imogen felt the blush rise from the tips of her toes,
sweeping rapidly to the top of her head. His mother!

She could only manage a disgraceful: 'Oh,' before she succumbed to the twinkle in his eyes and bubbled into laughter. 'Oh,' she repeated more firmly. 'Well, in that case, Mr Beaumont, yes, I'd be delighted to have lunch with you . . . and Lulu.'

'Good.' The word was briefly spoken. He waited until she picked up her things and then held out his hands. Imogen accepted their grasp and allowed herself to be helped up the short, sharp incline, and as she slipped on her sandals, observed rather apologetically:

'I hope you're not thinking of going anywhere too grand. I'm not really dressed for dining out.'

'They do an appetising lunch at the local Country Club, a few miles down the main Lynn road, and don't worry, you look delightful.'

Imogen straightened, hoping her colour could be mistaken for bending down. 'That sounds lovely,' she replied, and they began to walk across the undulating dunes, the happy Lulu racing on ahead, giving one or two short barks every now and then, her head coming round periodically to check they were following. From the dunes they trod a narrow path through some scrub which led to a gravel track, gradually widening into a road of inferior quality. Parked on one side was the red Ferrari. Lulu jumped into the narrow space at the back, declaring her territory. As Nat Beaumont opened the passenger door for Imogen to slip in, he said:

'Perhaps we should be introduced more fully? You know that I am Nathaniel Beaumont, whereas I only know you as Imogen,' and he shut the door smiling down at her.

'Adair. Imogen Adair.'

His smile deepened. 'Imogen Adair.' He rolled his tongue round the name delicately. 'Well, Imogen

Adair, shall we go?'

She found herself smiling back, nodding slightly, and watched as he walked round, easing himself behind the wheel. Afterwards Imogen was to realise that that was the moment she could have answered: yes, anywhere, if you promise to stay with me.

The Country Club was pleasant, the meal enjoyable. Coming away, the wind lifting her hair as the sports car raced along, Imogen remarked:

'You don't look like a farmer, somehow.'

He turned his head for a brief glance and grinned. 'I'm not. My grandmother was the descendant of the last Caffrey farmer. She married a Beaumont but inherited the farmhouse and land. We had a bailiff for a while and now the land is leased to various people—the Hunts, for example. We've kept the paddocks and still have some land for our use, two horses in the stables and a few chickens. A married couple live in a cottage on the estate, she sees to the house, he looks after the horses and gardens. Even though we're Beaumonts the place will always be called Caffrey's.'

'And your mother? Does she . . .'

'Good lord, no. My dear mama wouldn't last a week in the country.' It was easily said, but beneath the lightness Imogen detected a hint of disparagement. 'She has a flat in London, but as I told you earlier, she's in New Zealand at the moment, visiting one of my sisters.' As he swung the Ferrari into the Hunts' gateway, she asked curiously:

'If you're not a farmer, what do you do?' and then: 'No need to drive right the way down. It's a pleasant walk.'

'Rightio.' He turned the wheel, leaving the car slanted towards the road, before answering her. 'I work in the theatre.'

Surprise filled her voice. 'Really? You're an actor?'

'Good lord, no. I direct,' and seeing the surprise, he mistook it for ignorance, adding: 'Plays. In the theatre, or television.'

'Yes, I know.'

As she walked down the long drive to the house Imogen was disturbed at how disappointed she was that he had not made further arrangements to see her again, and then shrugged, laughing at herself. A man like that would not be short of female company, and after all, he had only asked her out to lunch because Lulu had wrecked her sandwiches. Yet that was not quite the whole truth, she knew. They had talked mostly of Norfolk, Nat questioning the places she had visited, telling her more of the history of the area—he was well informed, and she was sure he had enjoyed himself as much as she had.

The telephone rang the following day and Mary Hunt called Imogen to it, her eyes twinkling with amusement as she announced that it was Mr Beaumont of Caffrey's, observing with shrewdness the quick flush that came to her young guest's cheeks.

'Imogen? Nat Beaumont here. What do you mean by pretending to be a horticulturist? I've just caused Mary a great deal of amusement. What are you doing, if not working?'

Smiling into the phone, Imogen replied: 'Recuperating from glandular fever.'

'Poor you! I must say you don't look ill.'

'Oh, I'm much better, although I still get tired if I do too much.'

'Would it be doing too much if you helped me spend a few days' holiday?' His voice held a teasing quality and the breath caught in her throat as she answered:

'I'm sure it wouldn't.'

'Good. I thought we'd drive over to Scolt Head, it's part of a bird sanctuary, so we'll leave Lulu behind! Can you ride, by the way—or sail?'

'I can ride, but boats are a mystery.'

'I shall have to turn teacher, then, for I thought we'd go on the Broads if the weather holds tomorrow. I'll be with you in an hour.' He hesitated and then asked mildly: 'By the way, what do you do for a living, or is it a deadly secret?'

'It's not a secret, although I hesitate to tell you in case you think I'll ask you for a job. I'm an actress.'

'Good lord! What a small world.'

'And one which we shall totally ignore, to convince you that I don't need a job!'

'Very well. In an hour, then?'

'In an hour.' Racing up the stairs to her room, for once not panting out of breath, she realised that she was, indeed, getting over her illness, but the sparklingly alive face she presented at the mirror while she tried to tame her unruly hair was not due solely to good health.

There followed for Imogen a period of growing happiness. The days passed companionably, filled with laughter and intelligent conversation. Days were spent on Nat's small yacht, which he kept permanently moored on a stretch of privately owned water. He was an experienced sailor and often raced, crewing for a friend or vice-versa, and on the *Pandora* Imogen began her lessons on how to become a competent crew member. They explored the countryside, on Nat's part re-seeing Norfolk and gaining pleasure from showing it off to Imogen, now thoroughly captivated, both by the land and by her guide. If he knew, Nat did not show it, and she began to despair that it was purely friendship he wanted from her.

As she was such a novice at sailing it pleased her to be able to show her prowess on the back of a horse. There were two animals in Caffrey's stables, which were kept shining and clean by Jack Knut, whose wife Rosa was housekeeper for Nat. They were an industrious couple and obviously devoted to Nat, and the house, stables and grounds were lovingly kept.

Caffrey's was a beautiful place, old and mellow, full of good, solid furniture, and once expensive furnishings that were now a little worn but still clinging to an age of graciousness. It was a family house, and obviously too big for one man, and equally obvious that Nat loved every brick and stone of it.

They rode every day, Nat on a big grey called Bayard and Imogen on a sweet-tempered strawberry roan called Briony. As in everything he seemed to do, Nat was a competent horseman, sitting strong in the saddle, completely master of the mettlesome Bayard and yet treating him with gentle hands on the curb. The first time they went out together he watched Imogen and Briony with keen scrutiny, but once he was assured that she was safe and in control he eased his vigilance.

Coming back from a stiff canter across the pastures, they slowed down to walk the horses through a thin wood, taking a short cut back to Caffrey's.

Nat said suddenly: 'Wait, Imogen . . . your girth needs adjusting. Want to get down and walk through here?'

She nodded and swung herself from Briony's back, landing lightly on the dry, springy ground. While Nat fiddled with the girth she spied something colourful in the undergrowth and pushed her way through, eager to see what it was. She had not gone very far before she was well and truly caught up in a bramble bush and the more she tried to free herself, the more tangled she became.

Muttering with impatience, she was obliged to call for Nat, who secured the horses and came to the rescue. He grumbled goodnaturedly as he pushed his way through and carefully pulled aside the sharp-thorned stems which seemed to have a mind and a will of their own. As soon as he freed the one sticking tenaciously to her jodhpurs and started on the one on her blouse he was back again at the beginning.

Imogen began to laugh helplessly, trying to keep still at the same time, and he warned her:

'You be careful, my girl, or I'll leave you. This will teach you to leave the trodden paths and dive off into uncharted land. What were you after, anyway?'

'I saw . . .'

'Ouch!' Nat swore under his breath and muttered grimly: 'When I say go, dive towards me, will you? And be quick about it. Ready, steady . . . go!'

Two seconds later she was free and in his arms, and their shouts of triumph, high on ready laughter, stopped on contact and very slowly Nat brought down his head and kissed her. The whole wood seemed to go silent, then everything was back to normal and Nat was saying lightly:

'I think I deserved a prize after that torture,' and she replied, as easily:

'You were a pal to come to my rescue,' and the kiss was not referred to again, although Imogen could not forget it, and she suspected that Nat could not either. It seemed too much of a coincidence that she was packed back to the Hunts earlier than usual on the plea that he had work to do.

Imogen received another letter from her father in South Africa, telling her that everything was still going well with the tour. To Imogen, the Adair Company seemed strangely remote. Mary and Colin went about their business, giving no sign that they were aware of what was happening to their young guest. The sun, and plenty of exercise, had brought a bloom to Imogen, and her happiness gave her an inner glow that was unmistakable. Mary did voice her fears to Colin that she hoped Imogen would not be hurt, but he merely smiled and shrugged his shoulders eloquently.

Imogen, in fact, shared Mary's fears. Some instinct told her that Nat was holding back, that he was not allowing himself to care and that the kiss was a lapse on his part. Having reached his thirties he had steered clear of marriage and it would have to be someone exceptional to make him change his mind. Imogen, not normally lacking in self-confidence, despaired that it could be her. She knew, from the odd bits that he let drop, that his parents had not been happy together, but had made an effort for the sake of the children. Imogen's own childhood might have been a lonely one, but at least she had been happy. All Nat's had done was to make him into a cynic where matrimony was concerned. She tried to convince herself that she was happy with just his friendship, but after the kiss it merely underlined the depths to which she had fallen.

It was with a jolt that Imogen realised that Nat's ten days' holiday break was nearly over. They spent the last one on the *Pandora*. She was becoming quite a proficient sailor and there was just the right amount of breeze to take the yacht through her paces. Both of them were wearing T-shirts and shorts with plimsolls on their feet, and afterwards, sunbaked and pleasantly tired, they motored back to Caffrey's ready to devour hungrily a cold meat salad that Rosa had left prepared for them.

Before eating, Nat disappeared to shower and returned wearing long slacks and a clean shirt. Imogen was offered the use of the shower, which she accepted, and changed into a cool top with narrow straps and a pretty cotton skirt which she had thoughtfully slung into the back of the Ferrari in case they had stopped for a drink on the way home.

When their hunger had been assuaged, Nat carried the wine into the sitting room where they listened to Beethoven in companionable silence. Lying back in the huge, old-fashioned sofa, partly against Nat's shoulder, Imogen thought she had never been so happy before in the whole of her life. One of his hands moved gently up and down her bare arm while the other lay heavily across her waist. When the record finished and he did not move she twisted her head and murmured:

'Come on, lazybones, the side wants changing.'

'Who's calling who a lazybones? You're nearest,' Nat replied, and then the teasing quality of his expression changed, and with her smiling lips so close to his, it needed only the fraction of the thought before it became reality.

Afterwards Imogen knew that Nat had not intended the kiss to get so out of hand. It started off fairly innocently, fused and burst into flames, and sense on both sides scattered to the four winds.

It was Nat who came to first. His hands stilled and his lips drew away, and as the tension in him communicated to her, Imogen's eyes flew open.

'Nat? What is it?' she asked. He buried his face in the soft curve of her shoulder and murmured: 'My God, Imogen, I think you've bewitched me,' and he made to move away.

Imogen tightened her hold, the palms of her hands spread across his back, her voice shaken. 'Nat? Don't leave me . . .'

There was a long silence and he brushed his lips gently across her skin.

'My dear, I have many faults, but they don't include the pastime of seducing young and beautiful virgins.'

'Not even if she's a willing one?' Another silence and Imogen answered her own question, calmly: 'Especially when she's a willing one. You'll have to tell me some time, Nat, how you guessed. It seems a dreamy thing to be these days . . .'

'Imogen, don't!' He sat up and brought her with him. She would not look at him, but he sounded rather angry. What a hell of a way to spend their last evening together!

As she pulled the straps of her top into place, Nat said sharply:

'Imogen, look at me.' He waited a second and when she would not, put his hands either side of her face and gently turned her to him. 'I didn't want this to happen, and none of it's your fault . . . except that you're beautiful and I'm only human . . .'

'. . . and I'm more trouble than I'm worth.' She tried to make a joke of it, mortified and embarrassed. The front of his shirt was unbuttoned—her hands had been as insistent as his. 'It's all right, Nat. Good heavens, don't look so worried! You don't want to be committed and I quite understand.' Her composure was returning, thank goodness. She smiled brightly. 'And now, how about some of Rosa's delicious coffee?'

She felt his gaze still upon her and turned a wonderfully calm, friendly face. So this was the pain of love . . . the hell of caring too much. She smiled . . . this was what was meant by slowly dying inside . . . smiled teasingly. 'I promise not to attack you again.'

Nat looked grim, troubled. He stood and looked down, frowning, then said:

'Yes. I'll fetch it,' and walked slowly from the room.

On his return she was perched on a low stool, a volume of plays she had discovered in the bookcase open on her lap.

'I've found your Tom Stoppard, Nat. What an exciting writer he is!'

Shirt buttoned correctly, still slightly austere, Nat put down the tray, remarking: 'I think so.'

'I'd love to do one of his plays, but Pa favours the classics.'

'Come and get your coffee.' Nat took his own and sat in the armchair opposite, while Imogen sank to her knees on the carpet.

'There's nothing wrong with the classics, but a mixed diet is usually more palatable,' Nat went on, adding in puzzlement: 'Pa?'

How odd to be sitting here discussing Stoppard when suddenly my future seems to stretch forward into nothingness, thought Imogen.

'Mm? Oh, my father,' and she sipped her coffee and wondered whether she would get back to the Hunts without disgracing herself. There was nothing like offering oneself as a gift and having the gift thrown back at you. At least it was experience, and to an actress experience could be a living.

'Your . . . father? Adair! *You* are Gerard Adair's . . .'

'Daughter. Do you know him?'

'Yes. Yes, of course I know him—who doesn't, in our profession? I've even worked with him a couple of times in my extreme youth. And you're his daughter.'

'Well, don't sound as though it's unbelievable.' She put down her coffee cup and stood up. 'I think I'd better go now, Nat. Thank you for a lovely day. I hope you'll take me sailing again some time.' It was a polite hope. She knew he was going to put her out of his life. Nothing made a bachelor run so far as the love of a good woman.

She did not disgrace herself, and even managed to suffer the gentle kiss he gave her, before the lights of the Ferrari disappeared into the distance.

The days passed into a week. There were no telephone calls ... no letters ... but then she had not expected any, only foolishly hoped. Mary and Colin said nothing, but Imogen felt their concern. She took to going out for long walks and coming back, tired, but unable to sleep. Shadows began to appear beneath her eyes.

When she did see Nat again she hardly dared allow herself to believe it ... yet that was definitely Bayard, cantering along by the side of the dyke, and the straight-backed, fair-haired rider could be none other than Nat. He drew level with her, checking the huge grey and looking down at her. Silently, Imogen stood up and watched him swing himself to the ground, and as he came towards her she found her voice and managed a lame:

'Hello, Nat ... I'm picking early strawberries for tea.'

'Yes, I know—Mary said you'd be up here.' He was frowning slightly and there was a certain grimness around his mouth. He stood looking at her for a moment without speaking and then said simply: 'I've missed you, Imogen.'

She stared at him, her heart thumping madly.

'You have?' She gave a funny little laugh. 'I've missed you too,' and she went into his arms and he was kissing her and the strawberries scattered in all directions.

'We can't talk here. Will you come home, to Caffrey's?' Nat asked, and when she nodded, too happy for words, he fetched Bayard and mounted, reaching down to lift Imogen up into the saddle in front of him, her head resting on his chest, one arm holding her tight while the other held the reins.

'I don't think Mary knew whether to be pleased to see me or not. But being her landlord gave me an unfair advantage and she told me where I'd find you.' Nat laughed quietly, the corners of his mouth curving.

Imogen sighed happily, unable to believe that it was all happening, the soft velvet of his words embracing her.

'I'm only here for a few hours and then I have to drive back to London. We have to talk, Imogen.'

She tightened her arms round his waist and murmured: 'If you say so, but I can think of nicer things to do.' She felt his chest shake with silent laughter, savouring the intoxicating delight of being close, and Nat replied warmly:

'So can I, but we talk first.'

Jack met them in the stable-yard and took charge of Bayard, his eyes approving as they walked into the house together, arm in arm. Nat deposited Imogen on the sofa while he took a stance some yards away, leaning an elbow against the mantel, his eyes hungrily taking their fill of her. Imogen clasped her hands round her knees and returned look for look, the blood rising sweetly to her cheeks beneath the ardour of his gaze. Nat said:

'We've known each other for a ridiculously short

period and if we had any sense we'd wait, allowing us more time to get to know each other. But I have to warn you that I'm off to Australia in less than six weeks to film and I shall be there for some time . . . and I seem to be in rather short supply of sense at the moment. Or . . .'

'. . . we do what we both want to do, and that is . . .'

'Imogen! For goodness' sake go back there and sit down,' Nat appealed with despairing laughter. 'I can't think straight when you . . .'

Imogen tightened her arms round his neck and stretched up on tiptoes to kiss him, murmuring: 'Carry on, darling.'

'Or—we use the licence I have in my pocket, get married and spend the time together, here and in London, getting to know each other properly before I'm thrown in the deep end with work. I realise that you'd probably like your father to be present, but if we wait until he returns there'll hardly be time. If that's what you want . . .'

'No,' Imogen said emphatically. 'Pa will only demand a huge affair and try and make me wait. What about your mother?'

'She'll faint with the shock—she thought I'd never take the plunge. So did I, but the thought of you with someone else is not to be contemplated. You're mine, and don't you forget it.' Nat kissed her hard and masterfully. 'We can visit Mother in New Zealand on our way out.' He searched her face, suddenly serious. 'You're sure, Imogen?'

She looked up into his eyes, her face shining with happiness.

'Quite sure,' she said, and then he was holding her as if he would never let her go.

'More coffee, miss?' The waiter stood patiently by

her side and Imogen broke out of her memories with a startled jump.

'Oh! I'm sorry ... thank you, no. I've finished.' She scooped up the bill and collected her things.

Once more on the road, the Rover purring along smoothly, Imogen felt shaken and slightly sick. God! how the memories came flooding back, once you opened the dam, she thought bleakly.

Poss jumped down on to the front seat and began to clean himself. She stretched out a hand and fingered the fur between his ears. 'You never did take to him, did you, Poss? Jealous, I suppose.' She sighed, without realising she did so. Poss had not been the only one to be jealous. She frowned, saying crisply: 'So what if he's come back? He still thinks I've no mind or will of my own and I still think him an arrogant, charming bastard.' The tarmac was covered for a few more miles before she observed scornfully: 'And in one way he's right! I am weak. I must be. How else can you describe someone whose heart turns over the minute he smiles? Whose flesh leaps to life the minute he touches? Who only has to hear the sound of his voice and her darned heart flaps like a dying fish!'

Poss was not interested until he heard the word 'fish' and then his head lifted, ears alert.

'Life's too confusing, Poss.' Imogen gripped the steering wheel. 'When I'm finished at Queensbridge I'll start divorce proceedings.' Her face clouded with anger. 'How dare he stand there and say that being married to me suits his purpose! I'm damned if I'll serve any good purpose for him!'

The signpost to Queensbridge loomed up in the distance and she swung the Rover round the bend with rather more speed than was absolutely ideal.

She relaxed her foot on the throttle.

That's what anger makes you do, she told herself with a degree of despair. It makes you say things that were better left unsaid and it makes you do things that were better left undone. And it makes you drive carelessly. So. She would dispense with the anger.

The city boundary came into view announcing 'Queensbridge welcomes careful drivers.'

Her lips twitched and the dimples appeared, and she declared:

'It's a good job I can still laugh. Take a look at Queensbridge, Poss. We're about to take the place by storm!'

CHAPTER FOUR

'All the world's a stage'

IMOGEN did not make for the Carlyons' house, Treetops, but took the main road into the centre of the city. Queensbridge Civic Theatre, familiarly called the Queen's, was an integral part of a huge modern shopping precinct. Imogen found a place to park and made her way through the Town Hall Square and presently climbed a flight of stone steps and stood in front of the theatre.

It was red brick and architecturally plain, with nothing to commend itself from the outside. Inside was another matter. Inside there was the most up-to-date equipment any stage director could dream of and one of the largest stage areas outside London. The high standard of productions and original thinking had made the Queen's a byword in the profession.

Imogen did not go inside. Adam had promised to show her round and she was content to just stroll along, reading the billboards of past and future productions, lingering before the one for *As You Like It*. She shivered, whether from excitement or for the fact that her suit jacket was not for dreaming in, in the cool March air, and giving the theatre one last look she walked briskly back to the car and set off for Treetops.

Rehearsals were not to begin for three days and during that time Imogen and Poss both settled into Treetops with the ease of being long accustomed to adapting to different places. With Adam away in Paris on business, Liz and Imogen were thrown together more than they had ever been before. Imogen found a great delight in helping and playing with the children and she began to unwind, not realising until it was over that the Adair season just finished had been a particularly demanding one.

For Liz these few days showed her another Imogen, one with a much stronger sense of character than she had previously supposed. She had always liked her, but realised that she had been shadowed by the strong, vigorous personality of her father. Now Liz found that out of Gerard's orbit the unassuming Imogen was really a bright and intelligent girl in her own right and, from the things Liz gleaned, it appeared that Imogen's was the hand that made the Adair company run smoothly and efficiently.

'Was your mother an actress, Imogen?' The question was out before Liz had time to think whether it should be uttered or not.

Imogen lifted her head, knife poised to slice the apples for the pie Liz was making. 'Oh, no. She came from Dorset. Pa was playing at Bristol and met her while she was there on holiday.' She smiled. 'It was all very romantic. Love at first sight! She was extremely beautiful and Pa was handsome in those days—he still is, really.' She fingered the locket round her neck and opened it for Liz to see. 'I'm not like either of them.'

'I wouldn't say that,' protested Liz, eyeing the double portraits intently. 'You have your mother's shape of face and eyes, and your father's mouth— not forgetting his talent.'

Imogen gave a laugh. 'I only wish I had! I'll never be as good as he is.'

'I don't see how you can say that. At twenty-five you can hardly compare yourself to Gerard, who's had years more experience. Perhaps the time is right for you to work away from him for a while. Coming to the Queen's might turn out to be good for you.' Liz shrugged. 'Sometimes we feel that our parents expect too much from us, even when they don't.'

Nibbling a piece of apple, Imogen nodded, saying absently:

'Someone else said that to me. Even went so far as to say that Pa was holding me back, which was ridiculous. I've been in work ever since I was sixteen, unlike some.'

'Who was it?' asked Liz curiously, interested in who had the temerity to criticise Gerard.

'Mmm? Oh, no one of importance,' and she took satisfaction in saying the words, the image of Nat's cold, angry face before her. She handed over the apples and watched Liz cut the pastry. 'Mother died when I was three . . . I can't remember her.'

'How did Gerard cope with you and a career? It must have been difficult.'

'Yes, it must have, but he never made it appear

so. I went with him everywhere. He was marvellous.'

'And your schooling?'

'Pa taught me at first and then I had private tuition—you can always find someone willing to come out of retirement for a few hours a day. Now and again the authorities checked up, but I was a good student—I knew Pa wouldn't be allowed to keep me if I didn't try hard at my lessons, so I was always able to satisfy them. I took my exams and passed them and persuaded Pa that I didn't want to go on for further studies. I knew the stage was for me, what was the point? I became general dogsbody in his Company, learned everything from top to bottom, and Pa was strict. After a bit I was allowed a few lines and did my acting apprenticeship the usual hard way—by experience! I've been very lucky.'

Liz crimped the pastry edge and put the pie in the oven. Smoothing her floury hands down her apron, she considered her friend thoughtfully. What a mixture Imogen was! She had had a sheltered and protected upbringing, even allowing for the unconventional surroundings of theatre life, but apart from having a strong hero-worship of her father she was amazingly well adjusted. She asked:

'What about relations?'

Imogen began to dry as Liz washed their cooking utensils. 'We haven't any, at least, none we keep in contact with. Pa was an only and his parents died before he met Mother. As for Mother's people, they didn't want her to marry an actor. They were farmers and thought Pa came from another planet. I suppose they might have patched things up if Mother had lived, but Pa was still uptight about them and moving about all over the place made it more difficult—or easier, whichever way you look at it.'

'Aren't you curious about them?'

Imogen thought for a moment. 'I suppose I am, if I'm honest, but if they didn't want to know Pa they can hardly want to know me. I suppose that's what I can't forgive ... they'd have been a family for Pa. At least, with Mother gone, he had me.' She lifted her face to the window and gazed out with slightly wistful eyes. 'I've never allowed my curiosity to grow, out of loyalty to Pa, but in my low moments I admit to thinking it would be nice to belong to a family.'

Liz, coming from a large and loving family herself, could associate with the hint of regret in her friend's voice and said quickly and cheerfully:

'You can have a share of mine ... and working on a play can be like being part of a family, can't it? I'm sure you're going to get on well with our lot, they're a good crowd. You'll meet them all tomorrow.'

Imogen's face lit up. 'Yes, I can't wait to get started. A lovely theatre, a super part and working for Adam! I only hope I won't let him down.'

Liz seemed about to say something and then stopped.

The next morning Adam phoned to say he had been delayed on the flight in from Paris and he had gone straight to the theatre. After having spoken with Liz, he transferred to Imogen.

'Imogen, I want to have a word with you, but not over the phone. Can you hop on a bus, Elizabeth will tell you which one, and come in earlier than rehearsal call?'

'Yes, easily,' Imogen assured him. 'I'll come now.'

The bus route into the city was straightforward. Imogen got off at the right stop and quickened her step as she cut down a side road and approached the theatre from the back way.

Her pace slowed and finally halted as she sighted the blue Mercedes parked next to the white BMW of Adam's. She told herself that there must be hundreds of blue Mercedes on the road, but even as she tried to persuade herself that this one was not Nat's, she knew deep down that it was. As she came nearer, a sticker on the back window showing a view of the Opera House and Sydney Harbour was merely confirmation.

Imogen stood looking at the sleek lines of the beautiful car. Her reflection stared back at her from the window, the blank look replacing the one of excited anticipation of only a few minutes ago. She shivered, thrusting her hands into the slits of her jacket pockets. The cherry red jumper and dark navy cords should have been warm enough and the navy jacket was windproof, but she still shivered.

As she turned on her heel and made her way to the theatre manager's office she was asking questions of herself that were unanswerable, although the glimmer of a suspicion was showing, too awful to contemplate.

One of the secretaries greeted her in the outer office.

'Miss Adair? Do come in. Mr Carlyon sends his apologies, but he's been delayed for a moment. Will you take a seat while you wait?'

Imogen murmured her thanks and settled herself in a chair when the door swung open and Nat strolled in. The secretary leaped from her place at the typewriter to greet him enthusiastically.

'Good morning, Mr Beaumont—I'm afraid Mr Carlyon is delayed.' She was all of a twitter, and when Nat smiled at her she became a victim for life.

'Not to worry, I've just this minute seen him.

Actually, I'm looking for . . .' he turned his head and spied Imogen, trying to be invisible in her corner. 'Ah, here she is. I've come to collect Miss Adair on his behalf.' His eyes rested on Imogen thoughtfully for a moment and then returned to the secretary who was now handing over some letters, saying:

'These have come through the post, Mr Beaumont, and Mr Edwards has gone with his men down to the rehearsal room with Sadie Jones, and the carpenter was also looking for you, but he said he could wait.'

Nat said: 'Thank you. Give me twenty minutes and then anyone who wants me will find me down at Ross's,' while he flipped through the envelopes. That done, he turned to Imogen. 'Hello, Imogen. Adam wanted to take you round, but as you've heard, he's held up. He says will I do instead?' The tone was politely friendly and Imogen took her cue. Rising to her feet, she replied:

'Yes, of course,' and giving the secretary a farewell smile, allowed herself to be escorted out of the office.

As she walked down the corridor by his side she was remembering her heated avowal that she wished he would go away and stay out of her life for ever. No wonder he had found that request amusing, when she had just told him that she was coming to Queensbridge. He must be enjoying her discomfort, she thought bitterly. Well, she would jolly well disappoint him! And on that avowal her chin took on a determined tilt as she resolved not to let his presence throw her.

They passed through the foyer and attracted some curious looks from a group queueing for tickets at the booking office, and Imogen was not foolish to suppose they were directed at her. Nat's deep tan and sun-streaked hair were bound to cause interest in a country that had just gone through a bad winter. Dressed casually in grey and black, a cord jacket slung over one shoulder, he could hardly be accused of seeking attention, yet he still made a striking figure.

Their trip round the theatre was methodical and instructive. Imogen asked pertinent questions which Nat answered skilfully. She saw the large main auditorium and the small studio tucked away in the attics, and she came to realise what an alive and productive theatre the Queen's was—even the foyer space was being set up for a lunchtime performance of poetry and music. The citizens of Queensbridge were lucky in their artistic director, Adam Carlyon. Nat, it seemed, agreed with her, for having related plans for a 'new writers' club he went on:

'Adam encourages amateur groups with a festival of one-act plays each year, and at least three times a year has visiting ballet companies. This place is flourishing because it's active and forward-looking.' He brought up his wrist and glanced at his watch. 'We'd better go. You do know that rehearsals aren't actually in the theatre? Unfortunately, what the Queen's hasn't enough of is floor space. We're using the ground floor of Ross's warehouse, just down the street. It's not far.' He pushed open a door and Imogen found herself blinking in the daylight, the noise of the traffic sounding loudly in her ears.

'If you show me, I'm sure I can find my own way,' she said, probing for information.

Nat gave her a swift glance and a laconic: 'I'm due there myself.' And that was that.

As Nat said, it was not far, and they walked the rest of the way in silence. Imogen was too busy thinking to bother with any casual chit-chat. Nat was somehow involved with this production of *As*

You Like It and she was wondering frantically in what way, as well as who was this Mr Edwards that the secretary said was already there with his men. What men?

The rehearsal room seemed full of people and, what was more surprising, cables and television cameras. The noise was tremendous, the volume fading slightly as eyes were projected to the new-comers.

Nat's attention was immediately claimed by a man with headphones draped round his neck and cutting him short, Nat said briefly: 'Imogen, this is Jake Edwards—Jake, Imogen Adair.'

Curious, Imogen shook hands, but as the man was only interested in being allowed to speak to Nat she then firmly turned away, to be rescued from uncer-tainty by a small, tubby girl with an attractive freckled face and curly brown hair.

'Hi! I'm Sadie Jones, A.S.M. I think you must be Imogen Adair, our Rosalind, am I right?'

Imogen smiled and nodded her agreement, her fingers tightening on the copy of the script in her hand. She liked the look of the assistant stage manager, she seemed friendly, and a friend was someone Imogen could do with among this sea of faces.

'Come and meet the rest of the mob,' Sadie sug-gested, and as they began to walk across the room, which was a large rectangle, with bare windows, wooden floorboards and painted brick walls, she added: 'Recognise anyone you know?'

The only two faces that stood out in Imogen's fleeting appraisal was the redhead's from the night of the gala and an actor's who had played a season with the Adair Company once. Imogen had time for a second look at the redhead and a quick smile for

the actor before the doors swung open and Adam
breezed in. The chatter died down expectantly as he
made his way to Nat, spoke, shook hands with Jake
Edwards, said something that made the three men
laugh and then broke away to the centre of the
room.

' 'Morning, everyone. Sorry I'm late. I suppose
you're all wondering what the cameras are set up
for. I'll satisfy your curiosity by telling you that the
man over there with the headphones is Jake
Edwards, who, as I'm sure you all know, is the man
behind *Arts Diary* which goes out on Sunday evenings. He's doing a profile on my very good friend
and colleague, Nathaniel Beaumont, whom I've
managed to persuade to come and direct *As You Like
It* for us. Consequently all of you involved with the
play, to some degree, will be part of that profile on
Nat.' He paused and smiled, looking in the direction
of Nat, who was sitting on the edge of a table, arms
folded, gazing absently down at his shoes. 'I'll not
eulogise on his theatrical history—if you don't know
it, then you don't read enough. Suffice it to say that
we're lucky to have him with us and happy to be
part of his programme.'

Nat lifted his head and smiled his thanks for
Adam's comments. Imogen heard whispered sighs in
the feminine group around her, caught a murmured:
'What a dish!' from someone and then Adam was
speaking again.

'This must be somewhat of a surprise, my aban-
doning you, and I'm sorry I couldn't let you know
sooner, but although I had Nat Beaumont's consent
a few weeks ago, my own affairs proved more tardy.
I'm leaving you in good hands, however,' and his
eyes, passing round his company, rested briefly on
Imogen. She was thinking: Poor old Adam! What a

quandary I put him in. Going on and on about
looking forward to working for him and all the time
he knew there was a possibility of me being disappointed. She smiled to let him know it was all right,
even though it was not, and he gave the slightest
hint of a nod, his eyes moving on, finishing at the
figure by the table, suggesting:

'Nat—will you take over as from now?' and Nat
said:

'Thank you. Let's gather round and look at the
set, shall we?'

From then on the technicians took over. Backstage
crew, scenic and costume designers, stage and lighting directors, all were introduced to the cast in turn
and the interchangeable set, comprising the Duke's
Palace and the Forest of Arden, was displayed for
inspection. Nat pointed out details with a pen as
pointer, answering queries with clearly defined
answers, creating an impression of someone who had
every possible detail accounted for. Drawings of
costumes, wigs and hairstyles were passed round and
discussed and a full rehearsal schedule given to each
person.

Almost, Imogen could disregard the fact that it
was Nat, talking, answering questions instead of
Adam, for all this was second nature to her, part of
her life, as familiar as breathing. She looked and
listened with deep interest, her admiration growing
for the organisation and planning that had gone into
the production so far—right down to such fine detail
as to what height heels the men would be wearing
on their shoes.

Almost she could disregard Nat. Almost, but not
totally. Her eyes rested on him as he was listening to
his stage director, one of his hands rubbing his jaw.
What had his thoughts been when he learned, acci-

dentally from her, that she would be part of his team?
Displeased and probably annoyed, but not upset.
The imperturbable Nat Beaumont would not let a
little thing like his estranged wife upset the organised
balance of his life.

Two large tables were now being dragged to the
centre of the rehearsal area and Sadie was organising
chairs to be placed around them.

'Come on, Imogen, don't stand about day-
dreaming, grab this chair!'

Imogen swung round, her smile appearing as she
exclaimed:

'Drew! How nice to see you again . . . it must be
five years. What are you doing here?'

'Orlando to your Rosalind.' Andrew Wymark
pulled out a chair for her to be seated.

'It *is* lovely to see a face I know,' confided Imogen
as he took his place next to her. 'I enjoyed your
Scottish serial, Drew. Have you forsaken television
for a while?'

Drew cast a mocking eye at the cameras. 'I
thought I had,' he admitted, and with a degree of
shock Imogen realised that they had been under
surveillance all the while Nat had been explaining
the set and introducing everyone. Now the cameras
were homing in on the read-through of the play. It
was silly to be surprised. This Jake Edwards would
be after the way Nat worked, his rapport with the
company, anything that would give a clue to the
man himself.

'What are you doing here?' Drew asked, and
Imogen explained in a quick whisper before being
silenced by Nat's arrival at the head of the table.
Sadie joined him, pen and notebook handy for any
notes he might want taken down, and there was a
general opening of scripts, clearing of throats and

scraping of chairs. Someone distributed saucers for ashtrays and then Nat glanced round the table and said:

'We'll read the first act. Be relaxed, take your time—just let's hear the story come through in as simple a form as we can.' His face broke out into a smile, one brow rose quizzically. 'Right. Shall we begin?'

Imogen had a few pages of grace and was able to sit and listen to her colleagues. She was nervous, extra nervous because of Nat. She was more glad than she would care to admit that Drew Wymark was playing Orlando, and he was perfectly cast in the part. Of medium height, brown hair grown a little longer than the norm for the play, brown eyes and the sort of face, gentle and romantic, that young girls swoon over . . . that was Drew Wymark. The fact that his looks did not tie up with his personality was only to be discovered off stage. He had a great sense of fun, bemoaned his face which, he said, denied him the chance to play a 'baddie', and was a joy to work with, being a hardworking, disciplined and unselfish actor. Imogen's knowledge of Drew was limited to work, for Gerard discouraged her showing any favouritism among the young men in his company, and the young men, in their turn, did not want to put a step wrong with the daughter of their boss. But she had always liked Drew and sensed his cheerful, happy-go-lucky character would be good to have around to take her mind off her problems.

No more time for speculation: scene two, the Duke's palace. The redhead, whose name Imogen now learned was Donna Campbell, was playing Celia, Rosalind's cousin and constant companion. Imogen gave a philosophical sigh. Ah, well, if she had to put up with the redhead, so be it ... and following her cue, she began to read.

They broke for lunch half-way. Drew turned to Imogen, asking:

'Have you any plans for food? There's a pub round the corner that does a good ploughman's, it's a favourite haunt for hungry thespians. Care to join me?'

'Thanks, I'd like to,' replied Imogen, stretching thankfully, adding: 'I found that decidedly nerve-racking.'

Drew grinned. 'It was rather. I wonder what Beaumont thought of us all? He isn't giving anything away, is he?'

'I suppose he wants to see what we make of it ourselves,' suggested Imogen.

'He has a good reputation,' Drew said thoughtfully, 'as a director, I mean.' His brows rose as they watched Donna cross to Nat and a few seconds later walk out of the hall with him. 'Off stage I don't know about—but our Donna will soon let us know, no doubt.' He laughed. 'She's soon got her claws into Beaumont.'

'I doubt we need concern ourselves. Mr Beaumont looks as though he can take care of himself.' Imogen felt rather than saw Drew give her an inquisitive look and slipping her arm companionably through his, she went on teasingly: 'Where's this food you promised? I know we're supposed to be languishing with love for each other in the Forest of Arden, but right now any languishing I intend to do is over food! Lead on!' and Drew gave a mock flourish with his arm and they joined a straggling procession of fellow actors with the same destination in mind.

After lunch the atmosphere was more relaxed. Cigarette ends and sweet papers graced the saucers and plastic coffee cups littered the table. When Imogen spoke Rosalind's final lines there was a slight pause and then there ensued an informal discussion as to the depths of the play, the breakdown of the characters and the aims of the production. Nat led the talk skilfully, delving into half-thought-out ideas, arguing amicably and refereeing differences of opinion and finally stating his own demands from the players simply and constructively while indicating that they would have freedom of expression unless it totally went against the policy line they were aiming for.

There was a good feeling among the company, Imogen could tell that everyone was as impressed as she herself was, and her admiration for Nat as a director was seeded and began its slow growth.

At five-thirty the rehearsal broke, some of the company hastening to snatch a meal before donning make-up and costume for the evening performance of the Neil Simon comedy that was just starting its run and doing good box-office. Others, including Imogen, brought in just for *As You Like It*, began to prepare for home. Drew rushed off and as the hall began to clear Nat called to Imogen:

'Can you stay a moment, Imogen, please?' before returning to his conversation with Jake Edwards.

Imogen's hard-won composure slipped a little at the request, but she murmured her: 'See you tomorrow,' to various friendly 'cheerios' while the company dispersed. Finally, Nat and Jake walked to the exit doors, still talking, Jake disappearing with a cheery 'goodnight', leaving Nat to click the doors shut, leaving the two of them alone together.

The room, long and narrow with a high ceiling, had the usual look of bleakness familiar with a place that five minutes before had been full of people and industry. Nat walked back across the wooden floor, his steps sounding hollow, and came to a halt in front of Imogen, sitting on a bench, waiting. As he came he shrugged on his jacket and the collar was half tucked in. Imogen found herself wanting to untuck it, a feeling she suppressed as being too familiar. Was it possible to be too familiar with ones husband? she wondered, the bizarre situation causing her a flash of derisive amusement, which died, nervously, leaving her with misgivings over this tête-à-tête.

'How do you think you're going to like it here?' Nat asked abruptly, and seeing Imogen's guarded expression, he amended the question. 'Perhaps I should ask: How do you think you're going to like it here, working with me instead of Adam?' and his regard was uncompromising.

Now we are down to the basics, thought Imogen as she said carefully: 'That's rather an unfair question, isn't it?'

'A loaded one, maybe, but one that needs to be asked and given a truthful answer,' Nat replied.

Imogen deliberated for a few moments. She felt vulnerable. She wanted this job badly for a number of reasons, and now, having gone through the reading of the play, she knew she was going to fight for Rosalind. He asked for the truth—she would have to give it to him in as palatable a way as possible.

She held his look, determined to meet his challenge head on.

'I'm disappointed about Adam, from my own point of view. It would be pointless to deny that I've always wanted to work for him, but no doubt there'll be another time. He's obviously involved in something he wants to do . . .' her voice trailed, inviting information.

'Yes, he is. Adam's been commissioned to translate a Bennett play into French—you know he's part French by birth? Then he's to go to Paris and direct it with an all French cast.' He waited. 'You haven't answered my question.'

Imogen swung away impatiently, picking up her script from the table. 'What do you want me to say, Nat?' The words burst out defensively. 'I've hardly had the time to get used to Adam not being involved!'

'You've had enough time to draw some conclusions . . . and I need to know them, if we're to go any further. I can't work with an actress who hates my guts to the extent that the play suffers. I don't need to be loved,' and here his lips twisted into a grimace of a smile, 'but I do need every single person to be one hundred per cent for me. One rotten apple affects the whole barrel, as the saying goes.'

Imogen's head came round on that, the colour rushing to her cheeks. 'You think I'd do that?' she asked, the shock showing in her voice. 'Make trouble?'

He shrugged. 'I don't know, do I? And I can't afford to take a chance. That's why I'm asking. If you want to back out, now that you find Adam's not directing, then do it. I don't want to have to find another Rosalind halfway through rehearsals because you can't take direction from me.'

'Perhaps I should ask the same thing in reverse?' retorted Imogen hotly. 'Perhaps I should ask if *you* would like *me* to go! It's pointless carrying on if your dislike of me is going to interfere with me giving my best. This play is as important to me as it is to you.'

'If you stay you'll be Rosalind, not Imogen Adair—or even Imogen Beaumont. I'm quite capable of dividing my professional life from my private one.'

The fact that Nat was so cool and rational made things worse. She found his opinion of her, or rather his doubts of her, so hurtful that for a moment she could not speak. She made a big thing of collecting her jacket from the back of a chair and while pushing her arm down the sleeve, at last, with a palpable effort, said: 'And you think I'm not?'

'That's what I'm trying to find out.' Nat leaned back against the table, arms folded across his chest. He gave the appearance that he was willing to stay there until it was all thrashed out. 'Personally, I don't think you are.'

The hurt disappeared and indignation took its place. What a low opinion of her he had! Her own pride in herself began to assert itself and her chin came up.

'You've always thought me a poor creature, Nat, so your judgement doesn't surprise me. I can't alter that, I know, but I will say this. Adam is jealous of the theatre's, and his own, reputation. I'm sure that if he appointed you in his stead then he must have an extremely high regard for your ability. If *he* has, I surely can respect his judgement and accept you as his choice.' She needed breath and took it, wishing she could read his face. 'You have an equally high regard for Adam's ability, haven't you? You've told me so. Can't you, in turn, accept his casting? He chose me, I can do it and I want to do it. Any direction you give me I can take! If you have any doubts and want me out, then I'm afraid you'll have to take the matter further with Equity, and the union can deal with it, because I'm not giving up without a struggle.'

Some indefinable expression flickered in the back

of his eyes, briefly. He said: 'Right. That's all I wanted to know.'

Imogen ran the gamut of hope and despair, watching him gather together papers into a briefcase before screwing the cap on to his pen and clipping it into place in his top pocket. The pen was one she had bought him and the fact that he still used it did not surprise her. Nat was too practical to get sentimental over a pen, even a silver one.

'I can stay?'

He paused, briefcase half open, and regarded her, one brow lifted consideringly. 'Yes. Under professional conditions I should say we could work together ... even though we can't live together.' His eyes mocked her.

Relief swept over her ousting the tension, leaving her curiously lightheaded. Before she could answer, always providing she could have found an answer, the outer doors burst open, the noise reverberating and sounding abnormally loud. Sadie bounded in, a bunch of keys dangling from her hand, to stop short, uncertain of what she was interrupting.

'Oh! Ready to lock up, Mr Beaumont?' she called, and looked with barely concealed interest at the two figures standing by the table, their heads turned to see who had arrived, frozen for a few seconds like statues.

Imogen swung on her heel, murmured 'goodnight' to Nat and walked swiftly towards the exit.

' 'Night, Sadie,' she said as she came near, smiling. 'See you tomorrow.'

Sadie made some reply and then Imogen was out in the cool, fresh air, taking a deep breath and letting it out slowly, revelling in the 'see you tomorrow!'

For a time back there she had wondered if there was going to be a tomorrow. As she made her way

back to Treetops she pondered on what had passed
between Nat and herself, replaying the scene word
for word, each expression examined until in the end
she had to stop, too confused by conflicting
emotions.

CHAPTER FIVE

'And all the men and women merely players'

'I KNOW you must have been disappointed about
Adam, but what do you think now about our lovely
replacement?' Liz's too innocent face turned towards
Imogen over the breakfast table as she paused before
spooning cereal into Victoria's open mouth. Her
daughter, waiting expectantly in her high-chair,
uttered a verbal protest and Liz obligingly spooned
another mouthful in, adding: 'My spies tell me that
all the females have succumbed to those green eyes
of his . . . grrrhh!'

Despite herself, Imogen laughed. 'I don't know
about that, but I do know he has a way of disarming
people that's so neat it oughtn't to be allowed. He's
got the backstage crew eating out of his hand, and
as for the cast . . .' she shrugged, '. . . susceptible
females aside, there's this feeling of being involved in
something that could be theatrically good. Everyone
can feel it. He instils this confidence in the play and
in us so that we're all working our guts out for him.'
She stopped short at the sight of Liz's face and protested: 'Now, Lizzie, don't start jumping to conclusions! I'm talking professionally.'

'I know you are . . . but can't this admiration for

Nat professionally spread over a little on to the personal?' and Liz's eyes twinkled encouragingly. 'Doesn't the sight of him do anything to your heart-strings?'

'You wouldn't believe me if I said no, so I won't,' Imogen quizzed her, 'and I agree he's a sight for sore eyes, but . . .'

'But what?'

'He's so secure in his own strength that I'd be scared I couldn't live up to him.' Imogen stopped, uncomfortable beneath Liz's surprised stare. She tried again. 'I mean, I think even when he's breaking the rules he'd be doing it decisively.'

Liz nodded. 'Single-minded, ambitious and a mite ruthless, someone once said of Nat, but I wonder if anyone can be that sure?' she went on shrewdly. 'I get the feeling that he doesn't allow himself to become involved in relationships, that this standing back a pace is to ensure he's not let down.'

'A man like that's bound to be let down. He would demand too high a price,' Imogen said flatly, but Liz did not seem to hear, she was busy mopping up Victoria's face and hands, and saying:

'Seeing you together the night of the gala I thought how suited you both were. I wish you'd take him on, Imogen. He's too nice to grow old alone.'

'Perhaps he wants peace in his old age, and anyway, he's not interested in me, so you'll have to stop throwing him my way, Lizzie. You're not fooling anyone, you know.'

Liz pulled a face. 'He didn't mind giving you a lift that night, surely?'

'No, I don't think he did, but no more match-making.'

'No more, I promise. I daren't anyway. Adam would scold.'

Imogen smiled, eyeing her friend with affection. 'Now don't tell me you're scared of Adam, Liz, for I won't believe you.'

'Not scared of him, only scared of losing his respect,' Liz answered simply.

Clever Lizzie, thought Imogen, rising from the table. Once respect was gone how could love remain? She banished such sombre thoughts and ran for the bus. As it bowled its way to the city Imogen could not believe that two weeks had passed by so quickly. Each new day found her eager to begin, a sense of belonging enveloping her as she swung through the warehouse doors, the immediate goodnatured badinage and lively arguments of her fellow actors making her feel one of them.

She had realised at an early age that her relationship as daughter of Gerard Adair of the Adair Company imposed restrictions, but it was not until now, when they were underlined by comparison, that the limitations were made to be so apparent. Here, at the Queen's, she was accepted for her own value, most did not even know of her connection with Gerard, and she did not enlighten them. Any friendships she made were not hung over by the knowledge that she might have influence.

Here her thoughts took an ironic turn. No one knew more than she just how little influence she had with the artistic director of the Queen's.

A friendship that blossomed and grew was with Sadie Jones, the assistant stage manager. Sadie had been working at the Queen's for a little over a year and her down-to-earth good sense and bubbling high spirits helped Imogen enormously during the initial period, resulting in a closeness that grew daily.

One lunchtime they finished their snack at the

theatre bar and began to make their way back to
the warehouse. It was a day when the camera crews
had been in all morning and Imogen remarked how
at home Nat seemed among them. Sadie agreed,
exclaiming warmly:

'He's a regular Jack Horner, is our Beau ... he
has a finger in so many pies! I mean, did you know
he has a degree in law?' Her voice showed her awe
at this fact. 'I tell you this, Imogen, I love working
for Adam Carlyon and didn't think I'd find another
like him, but Beau's a close contender. He's polite,
calm, considerate and brilliant.'

'Do you call him Beau to his face?' asked Imogen,
half amazed, half envious of Sadie's relationship with
her boss. Sadie grinned wryly:

'Actually, no, but all the backstage crew call him
Beau behind his back. It's so appropriate, isn't it?
and really pleases me that he puts the fluttering eye-
lashes gently but firmly in their place. No mixing
business with pleasure for Beau Beaumont.' She
pushed open the door for Imogen to precede her. 'I
wonder how he's stayed single for so long?' They
descended the stone steps to pavement level and
turned down the street. 'Probably too busy to get
married,' she went on, answering her own question
and not noticing Imogen's silence on that subject,
'but not for women in general.'

'How do you know that?' Imogen could not help
asking, and Sadie looked at her pityingly.

'Ah, come on, Imogen, there's nothing wrong with
the Beau's hormones! He's all man, lovey. The
grapevine is singularly uninformed, so he's discreet
... although it's come up with one or two meetings
with a solicitor.' She caught sight of Imogen's face
and stopped short in her tracks. 'Imogen, what's
the matter? Do you feel ill?'

Imogen gasped out a reassuring laugh and shook her head.

'I . . . it's stitch . . . just a minute while I catch my breath.' She stood still for a few seconds while the buildings and pavement righted themselves, Sadie watching anxiously. 'I'm all right now,' Imogen told her, beginning to walk again. 'Go on about the . . . solicitor.'

'Well, this one's supposed to be quite a looker. Tall, dark, well dressed . . .'

'A woman?'

'Well, of course a woman! Aren't you listening, you goof? Solicitors can be female, you know— women's emancipation and all that jazz. Anyway, he's been seen with her a few times, wining and dining.'

'He's been to lunch with Donna a few times,' put in Imogen, thinking: not a solicitor for professional advice, merely one for pleasure.

Sadie grinned. 'Our redhead's not getting any-where. What's lunch in the bar in sight of half the company? We'd all have heard pretty damn quick if she'd reached first base.'

Imogen was inclined to agree. Knowing Nat as she did, she thought he would be wary of becoming involved with Donna while working with her on a show. Nat liked his privacy and guarded it with zealous determination.

'I don't blame him steering clear of involvement here—theatre people are such gossips,' Sadie announced sagely. 'And yet it's pointless looking out-side for a mate. I mean, who do we meet other than theatricals? What chap from outside would put up with the hours, for one thing? You'd be forever wel-coming him home as he was kissing you goodbye! So there's hope for us yet with the gorgeous Beau.'

Imogen turned a sceptical eye on her friend, asking: 'What about Doug?' and Sadie dismissed her current boy-friend, a lighting technician, with a mischievous shrug.

'Doug's for reality—Beau's for dreaming!' She studied Imogen, her eyes narrowing speculatively. 'What about you, Imogen? You're singularly quiet about our director. Do you think he's the stuff dreams are made on?'

Imogen sighed inwardly. First Lizzie and now Sadie!

'Of course . . . but so is Robert Redford.'

'Yeah—but Redford's unobtainable, damn it, and Beau's there to be grabbed!'

Imogen reached the door first and paused, saying dryly: 'I'm sorry to dash your hopes, but I think our director will want to do any of the grabbing that's going.'

'You're right,' agreed Sadie. 'All the same, I wonder when the grapevine will cotton on that off the set you two studiously avoid each other like the plague?' and on that observant note she breezed in ahead, leaving a nonplussed Imogen to trail after her.

A few moments later Sadie would have had to retract her words. Nat's voice, coming from just behind her, made Imogen turn, surprised.

'I think this is yours. You must have dropped it.'

Imogen took the airmail letter from his outstretched hand.

'Thank you,' she said quietly. He stood looking at her and she felt uncertain, wondering why he did not move on. She said hurriedly, filling in the awkwardness: 'It's from my father,' and thought, he must know that already, you dope, as he's had to read the outside to see that it belonged to me, 'and I haven't had time to open it yet,' and she smoothed the crumpled blue form between nervous fingers, her eyes on Gerard's spidery writing.

'Really? Been too busy to read Daddy's letter? That *would* upset him!'

She recoiled as if he had struck her, her eyes flying to his face, but he was already turning away, becoming involved with one of the camera crew in the setting up of a scene.

Imogen slit open the letter, the brief exchange affecting her more deeply than she cared to acknowledge. That piece of sarcasm was the first personal contact between them since rehearsals began. There was also an element of truth in what Nat said, which did not help either.

She read the letter quietly in her corner, knowing she was not needed on the set. She absorbed the contents, smiling once or twice at a turn of phrase, gathering from Gerard's low-key style that everything was going well and successfully and that the critical reviews were tolerable. This last made her chuckle. A letter from Duggan a few days previously had quoted some of them and they were overwhelmingly flattering. When it was read Imogen put it in her bag and sat on, thinking.

Drew plonked himself down on the bench beside her and put a friendly arm round her shoulders.

'What's up, love? Bad news?'

She shook her head, smiling. 'No. Just thinking.'

'Rather sad thoughts ... can't allow that. Come out again tonight for a drink?'

Touched by his thoughtfulness, her smile deepened. 'Kind of you, Drew, but I need to work on the last act, thanks all the same.'

'Another night, perhaps?' Drew suggested. 'I enjoyed your company and would like to do it again.'

Imogen's eyes flickered past him to see Donna and Nat sharing a joke together. She returned her attention to Drew and said gently:

'I enjoyed myself too, Drew, and yes, I would like to do it again. Thank you.'

Sadie caught their eye and beckoned and as they crossed to the acting area Drew said conspiratorially:

'Act four, scene one is to be shot today, with Nat giving us direction afterwards. Now don't let the cameras bother you, love. Ignore them and concentrate on me, I'm worth concentrating on,' and so Imogen was able to meet Nat with a genuine smile of amusement on her face.

The scene went well, causing a few smiles from the rest of the Company watching. Nat came forward and gave Donna and Drew a few pointers before turning to Imogen.

'That's coming along nicely, Imogen. This division between Rosalind pretending to be the boy while trying to hide her love for Orlando has a fine edge. It's easy to become heavy-handed and upset the balance.' He frowned thoughtfully, looking at her and yet not really seeing her. 'I think you have the boy right—I like the way you occasionally clear your throat and deepen your voice. Perhaps you can bring the female out a little more in places . . . allow the wishful thinking to be more prominent . . . for instance, in the line . . .' he turned to Sadie who held the script out for him to look at and flicked through the pages, '. . . where Orlando says: "Then love me, Rosalind" your "Yes, faith, will I, Fridays and Saturdays and all" can almost blow your cover with the longing in it. Let the Rosalind in you speak those words . . . you can remember to be a youth on the next line.' He smiled encouragingly. 'See what I mean?'

Imogen nodded, taking his direction perfectly.

'Orlando must be awfully in need of glasses,' drawled Drew, and everyone laughed. 'Yes, you can all enjoy yourselves at my expense,' he went on reproachfully. 'Here am I, supposedly content to make love to a youth as a stand-in for the girl I love, when any idiot can see the feller's a girl!' He groaned. 'Not only complicated, but ludicrous as well!'

Nat smiled sympathetically. 'You do have problems with Orlando, and the only way you'll win is to play him as you are doing, so lovelorn that he's forgiven anything.' He paused fractionally and pulled a comical face. 'I'll tell you in all sincerity that it's perfectly possible to mistake a girl for a boy. I know—I've done it, and I don't need glasses! Right, let's take the next scene, shall we?'

Nat had not looked at her while he spoke and she was glad, for she was sure that her colour had come up. For some reason, those words spoken in jest had cut through her armour like a ruthless sword. She could not define why, other than they brought back the memory of their first meeting sharply to mind, showing that he, too, had not forgotten.

They continued working and when a break was called Imogen took herself off and found a table to herself in the theatre bar. Fetching a cup of tea, she propped the script up in front of her and tried to concentrate on a particularly long speech. She heard footsteps coming her way and ignored them, hoping for privacy. Not until they stopped and she resignedly looked up did she realise that it was Adam. Her resignation changed to welcome and he smiled down at her, saying:

'Hello, Imogen, may I join you? Want another cup?' He was back in a few minutes carrying two cups and seating himself opposite, went on: 'I hardly see you at home, do I? How're things?'

'Fine. The play is going to be fantastic—me, I'm not so sure.'

Adam grinned. 'You have the usual paranoia. If it's any reassurance, the little I've managed to see looks good, you included. You make a lovely boy, Imogen. I can't wait to see you in doublet and hose.'

'You men are all alike,' Imogen grumbled mildly. 'The only thing that worries me is not to end up like principal boy in a pantomime!'

'You won't do that. Beau won't let you.'

She replied in almost amused surprise. 'No, he won't, will he?'

'How do you like working for him?'

Imogen was glad she could be truthful. 'I haven't had much experience of other directors, as you know, but he's lovely to work with. He has the ability to infuse his own ideas and yet still leave us with our own individuality stamped on the performance . . . and his ideas! . . . the business he puts in—well, I wonder how he thinks of it, I really do. It all seems so simple and right, and yet I couldn't have thought of it.'

Adam nodded once or twice as she spoke, showing barely concealed pleasure as he answered: 'Good, I'm glad you're happy.' He leaned forward, elbows on the table. 'Gerard asked me to write and let him know how you're getting on.'

'Oh.' Imogen looked slightly apprehensive.

'Merely as a surrogate parent, you understand, not as a theatre critic.' He waited for her smile and when it came, went on: 'I can see for myself that you're enjoying the work. The only thing is, I shall have to mention that Beau has taken my place . . . and I wanted to ask if you'd already done so.'

Her colour deepened and Imogen gave a quiet: 'No, not yet.'

Adam continued to scrutinise her, and for one wild moment she wondered if he knew, his next words dispelling the fear.

'I know it's a difficult situation when personalities clash, but even Gerard admits that Nat Beaumont has talent. I realised when you first approached me about a job for you here that there was the possibility I might not be around, but I said nothing because nothing was definite then. I also felt that the job was the more important issue, not who was directing.'

Imogen covered his hands with her own as they lay on the table top. 'Poor Adam! What a trouble I am to you. I admit that I've been putting off writing that particular bit of news, but I shall now do so. It's a pity that Pa and Nat don't get on,' she paused, wondering what Adam would say if he knew the whole, 'but you know Pa when he gets a bee in his bonnet.' Her eyes were caught by a movement beyond Adam in the foyer entrance. A familiar figure was through the door and striding towards them. 'Here's Nat now,' she went on quickly. 'Don't worry, Adam. I'll write and Pa will have to realise that he can't control fate! A few good press cuttings might help!' and she smiled, released his hands and picked up her script, her eyes sweeping upwards to Nat, who was now at their table. He did not acknowledge Imogen verbally, merely gave her a measured look before addressing Adam.

'Are you ready for the reporter chap now? He's here, I believe, waiting for us.'

'Then we'll not keep him waiting,' replied Adam, smiling at Imogen as he rose, and she watched them walk away together, a feeling of depression sweeping over her. To what did she owe the glacial expression?

she wondered, and then, five paces away, Nat turned. She waited warily for him to speak.

'I suppose you'll be at Lizzie's birthday dinner party?'

She replied quietly: 'Yes. And you?'

He gave her a rather wintry smile. 'Me too. Lizzie doesn't give up easily, does she?'

'You could have refused.'

'So I could. Perhaps I'm a masochist after all.' He swung on his heel and walked rapidly after Adam. They reached the office door almost together. Adam went in first, Nat paused briefly to look back to where she was sitting, before he too disappeared from view.

Rather grimly Imogen collected herself together and departed.

Liz's birthday fell mid-week, but she planned to celebrate it by a small dinner party the following Sunday evening. Imogen's offer of help in the kitchen was refused as Liz's daily help was giving her a hand and staying on to help serve, but, Liz said, if Imogen wanted to be an angel she could walk the children and keep them out of her way.

An angel Imogen was, taking Michael and Victoria to a nearby park to feed the ducks. They returned, tired and happy, and Imogen was an angel a little longer by bathing and bedding them as well.

She was perturbed regarding the ensuing evening. Two other married couples had been invited and when she had tentatively suggested that someone else should make up the numbers to evens Liz was quite indignant.

'Why?' she demanded. 'It's my birthday and I've asked who I want.'

'But I don't want you to feel that just because I'm here I have to be asked,' protested Imogen.

'You don't consider yourself to be my friend?'

'Yes, of course I do . . .'

'Good, because so far as I'm concerned, you are. Really, Imogen, are you getting het up because Nat's coming? I apologise for any teasing I may have done on that score in the past and I promise you that you've both been invited as old and valued friends and nothing more. Now, come and look through my wardrobe and tell me what to wear.'

At least I've tried, thought Imogen, and went to give her advice. Regarding her own dress for the party, some devil prompted her to bring the pale grey chiffon out for an airing. Its style was undated and it suited her and she liked herself in it—three good reasons to wear it. The fact that she had worn it for Nat on one of their enchanted evenings out she decided mattered not one whit. He probably would not even recognise it. She heard the front door bell ring twice while she was putting the finishing touches to her face—she had read Michael's bedtime story to give Liz a chance to get ready first so that she could greet her guests—and was annoyed to find her hand trembling. She glared at herself in the mirror and muttered:

'And just who are you prettying yourself up for? Fool!' She walked slowly down the stairs, in no rush to meet her fellow guests. Suddenly the mess her life was in struck her deeply. Marriage was not the ultimate aim, nor right, for every woman, but she knew that she needed a loving partner to see her through her allotted days. On the small landing she stopped, took a deep breath and told herself to snap out of it and enjoy herself. Descending the final steps at a run, she entered the sitting room.

Liz crossed quickly to her as she hesitated on the threshold, and a swift glance told Imogen that Nat had not yet arrived.

'Here she is. Imogen, do come and be introduced. I've just been showing everyone my lovely present. The sly girl borrowed my children one day and popped them into a local photographer's. How she managed to get Michael to keep it a secret I'll never know. He's such a chatterbox usually.'

'He wanted it to be a surprise as much as I did,' Imogen broke in, feeling absurdly pleased at Liz's reaction to her present.

'Sherry, Imogen?' asked Adam, coming up from behind and handing her a glass, which she smilingly accepted.

Liz tucked her arm through Imogen's and said: 'This is Imogen Adair . . . Imogen, I'd like you to meet Olivia and Matthew Raynor. I was at drama school with Olivia, although she was training to be an actress, whereas I was only interested in backstage work, and Matt's an old friend of Adam's, also a director of some repute and rapidly becoming a famous playwright.'

Imogen shook hands with Olivia and found herself looking into a pair of lovely eyes showing friendly interest, and then Matthew was taking her hand and saying:

'I think I shall have to employ Lizzie as my press agent! Good evening, Miss Adair. We have met before, at a rather crowded reception at which your father was one of the speakers, but don't apologise for not remembering, it must be all of six years ago now,' and his face broke out into a friendly smile.

'Do call me Imogen, please,' begged Imogen, smiling in turn, allowing Liz to draw her attention to the other couple sitting on the sofa, the man rising to his feet as they approached.

'Here we have Zoe and Gareth Williams,' Liz announced.

For a second, Imogen's face showed a blank look of recognition and then she recovered and fixed on a polite smile. Zoe Williams. So that's her name, she thought, eyeing the brunette closely as she went through the motions of being introduced. Zoe Williams . . . three years ago, sleepily answering the doorbell at Nat's flat wearing his silk dressing gown and probably little else. Zoe Williams with the stunning legs and attractive drawling voice.

'Zoe is an actress and a fantastic dancer,' Liz was saying, 'and if you didn't see her in *Manhattan* last year you sure missed something!'

No handshake, but a smile—was it slightly ironic?—and a rather shrewd look.

'And this is Gareth, the only non-theatrical here tonight, poor man, but he's well used to it, aren't you, Gareth?'

'A Welshman is never outnumbered if he still retains the use of his tongue,' put in Adam dryly, and the man from Wales, short in stature but in no way diminished by his tall friends, smiled, taking her hand warmly into his own.

'Maligned, I am, Imogen, as you can imagine. I assure you that I can never find a pause to get a word in!' There was a universal outbreak of laughter at this and his dark, intelligent-looking eyes twinkled. His voice, raised in mock indignation, proclaimed his native lilt, and Imogen found herself smiling back, liking him instinctively.

As she quietly sipped her drink she observed the Williamses and wondered at the mating of the drawling, slightly mocking Zoe and the bristling, energetic Gareth. The Raynors were more easy to accept and their ties were strong. Seeing Matthew sitting on the side of Olivia's armchair and placing his arm companionably round her shoulders, their eyes meeting, and the small exchange of an intimate smile, brought a swift stab of envy.

Liz said suddenly: 'Imogen, did Nat say anything to you yesterday that he might be late tonight?'

Imogen shook her head and Adam observed gently: 'Something must have held him up, Elizabeth. He'll give us a ring, no doubt.'

'But it's not like Nat, he's usually so punctual,' began Liz, and then the doorbell rang. 'Here he is now,' she said, and went out of the room. There was a natural lull in the conversation and everyone heard her aghast voice as she asked: 'Nat, what on earth has happened?' and then sharply: 'Adam! . . . Gareth! . . . come quickly!'

The two men left the room at once and the others looked at each other anxiously. Voices were raised and the murmur of Nat's, calm and unhurried, heard in contrast. Imogen found herself compelled to go too, her heart pounding, knowing that Liz was not one to make a fuss over nothing.

As she reached the open doorway into the hall Adam was helping Nat off with his jacket, the sleeve of which was covered with blood, while Gareth was giving instructions to Liz for some boiled warm water and antiseptic before going out to his car. Nat seemed unmoved by it all and, apart from being rather pale, was his usual cool self.

'Hey, steady there!' The kindly voice of Matthew Raynor reached her from a long way off and his hands drew her back into the room, forcing her into a chair.

'I'm sorry,' she managed, feeling all kinds of a fool.

'Does the sight of blood upset you?' Matthew asked, urging her to take a drink.

'No . . . yes . . .' She could not explain—how could she?

'Sit still a moment, you'll feel better presently.'

'Shouldn't we send for a doctor?' Imogen asked, and Matthew smiled down at her, replying:

'Gareth is a doctor.'

Adam came back into the room, explaining: 'Not as bad as it looks, thank goodness. Missed the artery. A stone hit his windscreen and he had to smash it with his hand. He was overtaking at the time and had to do some fast thinking before he could slow down and brake completely. As it is he's dented a wing on a centre bollard, but luckily no other vehicle was involved.'

'What a good job Gareth always carries his medical case with him. Is he officiating?' Zoe asked calmly, and Adam nodded.

'Will it need stitching?' Imogen found her voice. It seemed steady enough, showing a normal, friendly interest. She discovered Zoe's thoughtful appraisal of her rather unnerving and concentrated on Adam's reply.

'Gareth's cleaning it up now, we'll soon know. Let's have another drink,' he suggested. 'I hope you can stand waiting to eat.'

Talk became a mixture of shattered windscreens and accidents and Imogen was able to refind her composure. Liz came hurrying in, her face concerned.

'How beastly for poor old Nat. Gareth's stitching him up now. It's the splinters of glass that's taking so long. Adam, Nat's determined to stay on, but he looks pretty grotty.'

'We must leave it to him, Elizabeth,' soothed Adam, handing her a drink before leaving the room.

'What do you think of . . .' Olivia launched the

conversation into a lively discussion of a new play and twenty minutes later Nat walked in, pale but composed. He surveyed the group, drawling:

'Good evening, everyone . . . sorry for hogging the stage like this—unforgivable of me, I know. Hope you're not all fainting with hunger,' and his gaze passed from one to the other, his expression mocking, rebuffing sympathy, hesitating fractionally at Imogen, before moving on.

'We're fine, apart from Imogen, who nearly fainted, not from hunger, but merely at the sight of you, wounded.'

Imogen's eyes flew to Zoe in protest, and met her cool but not unkindly stare and she felt the heat rise in her cheeks.

'The funny thing about blood is that it affects people so differently,' interrupted Olivia, smiling kindly at Imogen. 'I can stand anyone else's, but not my own.'

Imogen hoped that Olivia could see the gratitude in her eyes before she looked down at the drink in her hand, not daring to catch sight of Nat's face.

'Of course, you all realise what a romantic figure the wounded hero cuts,' mocked Nat, indicating his sling. 'Lizzie, my dear girl, happy birthday. There's a volume of Oliver Wendell Holmes in the glove compartment of the Merc, all for you. 'Fraid I forgot to bring it in with me in all the rumpus.' He put his good arm round her and affectionately kissed her. 'Hope I haven't completely spoiled your evening.'

'Of course you haven't,' declared Liz firmly. 'You're here, not too badly hurt, and that's all that matters. I'm afraid I'm rather sensitive to car accidents . . . Adam was nearly killed in one.' She hugged him fondly. 'I shall love my Oliver Wendell Holmes and when I've rescued it, I shall go and give the all-clear to dinner.'

Nat watched her go and then turned to greet the others.

'Olivia, my dear, how are you? Looking extremely well, marriage to Matthew obviously suits you.' Nat bent down to kiss Olivia before turning to shake hands with her husband. 'Congratulations, Matthew, on your play—I caught it just before it went on tour. Zoe, my dear, you're looking more beautiful than ever. I'm so glad you had your medic in tow tonight, he's proved invaluable.'

'Gareth has his uses,' agreed Zoe, smiling. 'Nat darling, what a gorgeous tan you have! How many broken hearts did you leave behind in Australia?' She rose gracefully to her feet and kissed him, tucking her arm through his uninjured one.

'I'm too much of a gentleman to tell you.'

Zoe laughed softly. 'I shall use my imagination.'

Nat looked down at Imogen and gave her a small smile. 'Hello, Imogen.' She returned his greeting, aware of her inadequacy to say more and of Zoe's bright, curious eyes devouring her.

Liz called from the door: 'Shall we eat?' and they all trooped through into the dining room.

The evening, for Imogen, proved surprisingly enjoyable. She was seated between Gareth and Matthew, intelligent and interesting talkers and both taking pains to draw her out. There was only one awkward moment round the table, when the conversation turned to Imogen herself, the role of Rosalind and then, quite naturally, on to her father. Matthew was saying some complimentary things about Gerard Adair and Olivia, hearing his name, came into the discussion, saying interestedly:

'You usually work with your father, don't you, Imogen? I suppose there wasn't much point you

going to America with him this time. Nice to be
working at the Queen's, though.'

'Gerard was all for you going, wasn't he, Imogen?'
Adam broke in quietly. 'He wanted her to see the
country,' he explained to the rest, and smiled, 'but
Imogen was determined to be my Rosalind and as
usual she got her way.'

'Except that she's Nat's Rosalind,' drawled Zoe,
from across the table, and that turned the talk nicely
towards Adam's reasons for handing over to Nat,
and from there it went to France and stayed until
they moved back to the sitting room.

Olivia tinkled on the piano softly while they
waited for coffee and Gareth wandered over and
finding a tune they both knew, broke out into a song,
proving himself to be a true Welshman, his voice
natural and unforced. When Liz arrived, carrying a
tray, she was followed by Poss, who stalked in at her
heels, his amber eyes staring round the room in a
sweeping glance, tail held high.

Olivia, coming to the end of the song, swivelled
round on the piano stool and exclaimed: 'What a
beautiful cat!' and she stretched out a hand to stroke
him. Poss suffered the caress and passed on, examin-
ing everyone in turn. When he came to Nat, seated
on the sofa, his long legs sprawled out across the
hearth, Poss stopped short.

'Well, Poseidon—and how are you?' Nat asked,
while everyone looked on with interest at the cat's
strange behaviour. The hair along Poss's back rose
and his tail began to wave angrily. Nat made no
attempt to touch him, merely eyed him with as much
interest as the others.

'How strange,' Liz said wonderingly, pausing with
the coffee pot. 'He's normally friendly. Don't you
like cats, Nat?'

'Mm . . .? Oh, yes, I like most animals. I'm afraid the boot's on the other foot, isn't it, Poseidon?' Poss gave a final angry flourish and turned his back on Nat, carefully threading his way to where Imogen was sitting, curled up on the carpet. Poss daintily jumped into her lap and after a few turns, settled himself down.

'The animal has some sense,' commented Gareth, grinning at Imogen, and Zoe asked: 'He belongs to you?' and Imogen nodded, very conscious of the sardonic gleam in Nat's eyes.

'If he were a black cat, and not this beautiful marmalade colour, we could suspect that he's a witch's familiar,' Zoe went on, and Nat drawled: 'Are you a witch, Imogen?' and she replied: 'Of course,' and then Gareth asked:

'Talking of cats, has anyone seen the new musical? I hear it's very good,' and the chat veered away from Poss and his reaction to Nat.

A little later Imogen turfed Poss out into the garden and bringing fresh coffee from the kitchen took a cup over to Nat. As she handed it to him, she murmured:

'You look tired . . . and in pain. Will you let me take you home, Nat?'

His brows rose. 'Won't that make the tongues wag?'

'Don't be flippant! You ought to be in bed.' Gareth was nearby and she claimed his attention. 'As his physician, Gareth, please tell him how awful he looks.' She kept her tone casual, in the manner of a concerned friend.

Gareth shot them both a look, taking in Imogen, unknowingly sincere, to Nat, coolly amused. 'I admit, Nathaniel, old fellow, you do not cut a fine picture of health,' he said at last. 'I shall give you pain-killers for tonight ... I suppose there's no chance of you taking tomorrow easy?' He pursed his lips. 'No, I suppose not. Very well, I support Imogen. Nat, go home to your bed.' He tilted a bright glance towards Imogen. 'I shall go and get the pills and you shall see that he takes them.'

Imogen searched Nat's face, her eyes questioning, and he reached forward to place his empty cup on to the table.

'Adam can run me home, it's not far. It's too late for you to be out on your own on the run back here.'

'Nonsense. I shall take Poss with me, he's as good as a guard dog, and it will spoil the party if Adam leaves.' She waited, seeing his reluctance, and said: 'Of course, if you're scared of your reputation ...' and she saw his eyes gleam and knew she had won.

Poss squatted on the back seat of Adam's BMW, ill at ease. Imogen needed Nat's instructions on the route, handling the car carefully but not timidly. She remarked once:

'If you need a car while the Mercedes is being seen to, the Rover is in Adam's garage, doing nothing,' and Nat replied:

'Thank you, but Adam's offered the BMW, if necessary.'

Finally pulling up outside a block of modern flats, she asked:

'Is this it?' and Nat nodded. 'You'll not forget to take the pills?' she added hesitantly.

'I'll not forget to take the pills.' He swivelled in the seat to look at her. 'You wouldn't like to come up and administer them personally? You might like to tuck me up in bed?'

'I don't think either suggestion will be necessary. We all know what a capable person you are.' She was furious to find her heart thumping away like mad. Really, she was impossible. Where was her pride, for heaven's sake? She went on coolly: 'You should have asked Zoe Williams to come with you if you wanted that. I'm sure she'd have been only too pleased.' She saw the gleam of his teeth in the half light and regretted her anger, knowing she had given herself away. She said quickly: 'Anyway, you still have the use of your right hand.'

Nat gave a considering nod of his head. 'Quite correct.' His arm came up and rested along her seat, his hand grasping the back of her neck gently. 'Did you wear this dress to remind me of happier times?' His fingers brushed the filmy chiffon softly. Imogen gave an uncontrollable shiver. 'Zoe recognised you, Imogen.' His voice was quiet and matter-of-fact.

'I know she did.'

'You wouldn't leave a name or wait, she tells me.'

'There seemed to be no point. Two's company, etc.' His hand was caressing her, almost casually, thoughtlessly, and she sat stiffly, her face turned resolutely to the front window, knowing he was watching her.

Now his hand was touching soft, smooth flesh and there was nothing casual or thoughtless about its movement, which had become gentle, deliberately sensuous. Imogen closed her eyes, emotion rising within her.

Nat asked gently: 'Why did you come, that day, Imogen?'

'Does it matter?' she asked wearily.

'Not really. We can't change what's happened in the past, can we? We can only learn from it.'

His voice was conversational, his hand hypnotic. Imogen swallowed hard. 'Please, Nat . . . don't.' It was a plea.

His lips touched her ear, he blew gently at a wisp of hair.

'Your heart doesn't want me to stop. I can feel it thumping away beneath my palm. You can't deny that my hand feels very much at home, Imogen.'

'I don't deny it.' The words came with a rush, harshly. 'I've never denied that my body was yours, Nat.'

There was a long pause and Nat gave a deep sigh, his voice regretful. 'No, you've never denied that, Imogen ... and we're both too intelligent to think that that's enough.' His hand lay warm, cupping her breast, his arm heavy yet comforting across her chest. The weight lifted reluctantly and his hand touched her chin, bringing her face round. 'It's a pity, isn't it?' he murmured, and pulling her just a little towards him, he kissed her, lightly yet lingeringly, his eyes holding hers all the time. His lips withdrew but his face remained close. She could feel his warm breath on her mouth.

Poss jumped up on to the back of the seat, pushing his head inquisitively between them.

Nat let her go and gave a bark of laughter. 'Okay, feller, calm down, I'm going.' He slanted Imogen a glance. 'Are you sure that damn cat isn't Gerard's familiar?' and then he was out of the car and walking up the steps and through the doors.

CHAPTER SIX

'We that are true lovers run into strange capers'

'THERE's no point me carting Nat to the theatre today, is there? Imogen has to go into rehearsal, so she might as well do it.' Adam looked pleased with the idea. 'You don't mind, do you, Imogen? Save me the journey,' and he tossed the car keys down on to the table and went back to the morning paper.

Imogen said: 'No, of course I don't mind,' because there was nothing else she could say, but the memory of the previous night was still with her, still teasing her senses and confusing her thoughts.

'What a good idea,' declared Liz, dealing with her husband's empty cup in between spooning egg yolk to Victoria and dishing up Michael's cereal. 'Every time I remember opening the door and seeing him standing there with his arm covered in blood, I feel sick.'

'Don't think about it, then,' advised Adam, from behind the paper.

'I can't help it. It was a shock.' Liz passed back the filled cup. 'A good job it was Nat's left hand.'

'He's left-handed.' Two pairs of eyes gazed at Imogen following this bit of news—Adam's interested, Liz's shrewd. Imogen found herself flustered. 'I think,' she added lamely, and began to spread butter on her toast.

'Good lord, you might be right,' said Adam, furrowing his brow. 'That will be slightly more of a nuisance.' He stood, moving to kiss his son and daughter, halting at Imogen's chair. 'Gareth left more pain-killers and instructions for Nat to see his own doctor. You'll have to use your powers of persuasion for him to do either, I suspect.' He dropped a kiss on the top of Liz's head and walked to the door, saying: 'I'm in the study.'

When Victoria had been deposited in the playpen and Michael had disappeared into the garden, Liz poured out another cup of tea for herself and Imogen and sat down, grateful for the respite. Poss stalked across the kitchen and sat down at her feet expectantly, and she leaned over and poured him some milk in a saucer, observing mildly:

'I didn't know Poseidon was his real name. How clever of Nat to guess.'

Imogen gave a reluctant smile and Liz replaced the milk jug and looked at her friend pensively.

'Do you want to talk about it?' she asked gently. 'If you do, I'll listen. If you don't, I'll not ask questions.'

Imogen said slowly: 'I think it might help if I do. It's all a bit of a mess, Lizzie,' and her friend answered dryly:

'It usually is, where a man's concerned.'

Imogen frowned and gave a short sigh. 'Half the trouble has been our upbringing, Nat's and mine, and the influence brought to bear on us. Do you remember when I was convalescing in Norfolk, three years ago?'

Liz nodded. 'When Gerard went to South Africa on tour without you.'

'It was an idyllic summer, hot, lazy days . . . it seems a dream now. We met quite by chance and Nat had some holiday due and we spent it together— all very correct, by the way. I fell in love with him, of course, and made it pretty apparent. I knew his views, his parents had made him cynical about marriage and he'd steered good and clear up to meeting me. I intimated that I'd settle for an affair, but for some reason he wouldn't take me up on the suggestion. I scared him off and he took to his heels. His own feelings were more deeply affected than I realised. It seemed, unbelievably, that Nat loved me too. Anyway, summer madness must have hit him, because he came back and asked me to marry him.'

'Imogen! You and Nat . . .?' Liz gaped and looked amazed, and Imogen smiled a little sadly.

'Married each other, right away, because Nat was going to Australia. If we'd waited for Pa to get back from South Africa there'd have been very little time, hence the rush. At least, that's why Nat rushed. My reasons for not delaying were more devious.' She thought for a moment, crumbling a morsel of bread between her fingers, before saying dreamily: 'I was wildly, deeply in love with him, Lizzie—you can imagine, can't you? It had never happened to me before and I could hardly believe that he loved me. I didn't let on that Pa was bound to raise Cain. He wouldn't have approved of any man marrying me, not at first, and I knew that a fait accompli was the best arrangement. What I didn't know was that Nat was Pa's bête noir.' She gave small groan. 'It was all much, much worse than I expected. Lizzie, for a long while now Pa's had a problem, a drink problem, which recurs every now and then, usually in times of stress. Duggan is marvellous with him and we've managed to cover up for him, I don't think it's known,' and Imogen looked enquiringly at Liz who shook her head, sympathy and surprise on her face.

'No, I'm sure it's not.'

'Pa's a splendid actor and a brilliant director. I love him dearly. He's been a marvellous father to

me and has loved and protected me, but every
parent has to learn to let go, and Pa won't. I
began to realise this in my late teens and I've only
had to take a stand over a few minor things because normally what he wants, I want too, so
things went fairly smoothly. Until Nat. You can
imagine, can't you, Lizzie? Pa coming home from
the tour and finding me married to Nat, of all
people. The drinking started up again, and I was
silly, I suppose, but I didn't tell Nat about that, I
knew Pa would have hated him knowing. If I'd had
the time I could have dealt with both Nat and Pa,
I'm sure I could, but there wasn't any time, only
two weeks, in which Nat was racing round with
last-minute details for going to Australia. To cut
a long story short, after endless arguments Nat and
I had an almighty row, when both of us said things
better left unsaid. The summer idyll exploded. To
Nat it was quite straightforward. If I loved him,
I'd go with him. As for me, I was torn in two, half
out of my mind with worry, sick with a kind of
despairing anger and hurt, that Nat thought me a
weak Daddy's girl. I tried to explain that if I
stayed behind, for a little while, I could get Pa
back on to an even keel, bring him round to the
marriage, which I knew I'd be able to do, and
then I would join Nat out there. But after this final
row I packed my bags and left.'

'But, Imogen, did Nat just go to Australia and . . .
forget about you?' Liz asked in some dismay.

Imogen shrugged and did not answer for a
moment. 'I suppose he did. As for me, two days
before he was due to leave I realised I couldn't let
him go without me. I went flying round to the flat,
all ready for a passionate reunion, and found a girl
there.'

Liz said softly: 'Oh, no, Imogen, how awful for you!'

Imogen gave a bitter smile. 'Retribution, indeed. I'd had my chance and muffed it. The place looked as though a tornado had swept through it. Beer cans and empty bottles, clothes half packed in two suitcases—there'd been quite a party going on. Through the open door I could see into the bedroom. Nat was asleep, he must have been out for the count, because he didn't hear the bell. The girl did. She vacated my side of the bed and opened the door, still half asleep herself and wearing Nat's dressing gown. Some scene for a reunion,' asserted Imogen dryly.

'Perhaps it wasn't as it looked,' began Liz, and stopped. 'Yes, well, we'll be realistic . . . but lovey, men can do that sort of thing and it doesn't mean much to them, you know.'

'My cool, rational logic tells me that, but my pride tells me he soon found consolation elsewhere. And I was too young to cope. I fled, and Nat went to Australia and apart from monthly cheques which I refuse to touch, he's not been in contact with me since. The gala was our first meeting in three years.'

'Has there been a divorce?' Liz asked tentatively, and Imogen shook her head.

'No. I guess I hoped . . .' She gave a self-mocking laugh. 'I kept hoping I'd hear from him. I couldn't believe it was all over. How stupid can you get? Nat wrote me off and forgot me.'

'I doubt that,' argued Liz. 'I've watched him looking at you, Imogen. He didn't forget.'

Imogen wrinkled her nose, considering this, and said thoughtfully: 'Perhaps not. There's still something there between us—certainly desire. But where's the respect?'

They drank their tea in silence for a while and then Liz asked:

'And you?'

Imogen gave a funny little smile. 'Me? Oh, I'm a fool. I still love him, despite everything. I'm older and time makes you see things more clearly. I'll get over him, don't look so worried, Lizzie dear. I needed to see him again, I realise that. I've decided to be me, from now on. Not Pa's daughter, or Nat's wife, but Imogen Adair in her own right. I've learnt my lesson.'

'What will you do?' asked Liz.

'I've had letters regularly from Duggan telling me Pa's well, no drinking. He *can* do it, and without me. America was a sort of trial. When he comes home I shall encourage him to give up the Company and act or direct for other people, much less responsibility. As for me, I shall get a divorce. Until I do, I shall never be completely free of Nat.' She laughed gently. 'Don't look like that, Lizzie.'

'But, my dear, are you sure that's what you want? Is there no hope for you and Nat?'

'I honestly don't know. We're playing cat and mouse at the moment. Sometimes I've had a feeling . . . Oh, it's still all a mess.' She grinned, genuinely amused. 'I think Nat is in a tangle of confused emotions as much as I am, and furious with me for it.'

'Why go through with a divorce, then?' Liz asked, bewildered.

'He might find he doesn't want one, if I do. And I might be wrong about Nat.' Imogen drained her cup and stood up. 'Bless you for listening, Lizzie. I feel better and not quite so confused in my own mind.' She began to clear the table. 'I liked your friends, last night. It was a lovely evening . . .'

'. . . apart from Nat's accident. Yes, I enjoyed it.'

'How long have Zoe and Gareth been married?'

Liz flapped the tablecloth at the back door, scattering the crumbs for the birds, coming back in to say: 'About two years. He's a lovey, isn't he? A Harley Street man. He adores Zoe.'

'Does she adore Gareth?'

Liz stopped to think. 'Yes. Yes, I'm sure she does. Zoe covers up all manner of things with that sophisticated veneer of hers. She always swore to us that she was going to marry money and she did, but I think for the right reasons. Zoe would never admit it, though. Hey, look at the time! You'd better go and pick Nat up. The pain-killers are on the hall table. I reckon you've a better chance of getting them down him than Adam!'

Ringing Nat's door bell twenty minutes later, Imogen hoped so, and seeing his face when he opened it made her determined to succeed. He was half-dressed and apart from looking ill, was extremely irritable.

'Oh, it's you. Where's Adam?' He stepped back and said bluntly: 'You'd better come in.'

'Thank you,' replied Imogen dryly. 'It wasn't my idea, but Adam's.' She crossed to the table, where there were remains of breakfast, and poured out a cup of tea.

'What's that for?' demanded Nat suspiciously as she handed it to him.

'So that you can take these,' she said calmly, bringing out the packet Gareth had left and tapping two pills into her palm. 'Doctor's orders.' She waited. 'We don't go until you take them.'

'You're becoming very wifely all of a sudden,' Nat sneered, 'and unless you'd forgotten, I have only one hand available, and that's already holding the cup.'

Imogen took the cup, dropped the pills into his

palm, waited until he swallowed them and passed back the cup.

'Satisfied?' Nat asked, and glared.

'For the moment. Are you intending going like that to rehearsal?' She arched her brows delicately. 'If so I doubt you'll get much work done. We have some fairly susceptible females around and the sight of your manly chest might prove too much for them.'

Nat scowled. 'If I'd known you were coming I'd have covered up. As it is, you'll have to put up with it.'

'Oh, I don't mind,' she said in mild surprise. 'I'm not one of the susceptible ones.' The scowl lifted and she caught the gleam in his eyes and went on quickly: 'Am I allowed to ask how you're feeling, and what sort of a night you've had?'

'You are. I'm feeling lousy and I had a rough night. I can also do without sharp-tongued, insensitive females who take advantage of a man's disability. Now you're here you can prove yourself useful.' He stalked into the bedroom and looked back at her. 'You can surely enter the wolf's den? I'm hardly in a position to do any harm to your maidenly modesty.'

Imogen followed him, saying: 'I'm a maiden no longer, remember? And do stop snarling. It doesn't scare me, merely makes me want to laugh. Is this the shirt you're going to wear? Slip your arm out of the sling and let's see if you can get it down the sleeve.' She waited while this manoeuvre was accomplished. 'Is that too tight or shall we need to slit it?'

'That will be fine.'

The mildness of his tone was more dangerous than the snarling. Imogen said quickly: 'Put your other arm through and I'll do up the buttons.' She was silent, concentrating on the buttons, ignoring the golden fuzz on his chest, the male smell of him. Her eyes flickered upwards to find him lazily contemplating her. 'You've cut yourself shaving,' she murmured, and then: 'Do you want a tie?'

'No, I do not want a tie, and if you come earlier tomorrow, you can shave me yourself.'

'I shall do no such thing. You won't be warm enough—have you a waistcoat, or a zip-up?'

'Two drawers down.' Nat seemed amused.

Silently Imogen fetched a tan suede waistcoat and helped him on with it, then retied the sling.

'What a lovely nurse you make, Imogen.'

'Better than Zoe?' She made her face mildly interested.

His eyes mocked her. 'Oh, much better than Zoe. She's definitely not nurse material.'

Imogen did not react further and returned to the living room, Nat following, his voice behind her saying:

'We're in good time. How about a cup of tea?'

'Not for me, thanks, but I'll pour another for you.' She did so and crossed with it to where he was now seated. She watched while he struggled to open a packet of cigarettes and putting the cup and saucer down on a small table nearby, took the packet from him. Taking out a cigarette she put it between his lips and as she struck a match, remarked:

'I thought you'd given up.'

He drew on it hard, eyeing her over the flame. Then:

'I have done.' His eyes narrowed as he watched the smoke rise. 'I indulge occasionally . . . when I'm in a snarling mood.'

'I wish you wouldn't.'

There was a long silence during which Imogen

wished she could have eaten her words.

Nat said in exaggerated surprise: 'I'm touched at your concern.'

Imogen swung away and answered in a spurt of weary anger: 'Oh, come off it, Nat. Of course I'm concerned. I wouldn't wish a lingering death on anyone.'

'I seem to remember you telling me once to go to the devil.'

'Quite likely, and you probably will without me sending you there.' She turned to face him. She was right, the over-gentle tone covered anger. She looked at her watch. 'Shouldn't we make a move?'

'I think perhaps we should.'

They walked in silence down to the BMW and as Imogen eased away from the kerb, Nat said:

'Did you enjoy yourself with Drew Wymark the other night?'

'Yes, thank you.'

'Mmm ... I never think it politic to become involved with one's leading man. Makes for an uneasy alliance should interest wane.'

Imogen said cheerfully: 'Oh, I so agree.'

'I shouldn't have thought he'd be your sort.'

'Really?'

'He has a reputation for liking the ladies.'

'I'm not surprised. He's attractive and good fun.' She gave him a brief glance before returning her attention to the road ahead. 'Just because you don't want me, Nat, it doesn't mean that no one else does.' And stick that in your cigarette and smoke it, she thought grimly. They were nearly in to the centre before Nat spoke again.

'Are you happy at the Queen's?'

'As happy as one can hope or expect to be.'

'Dear me, we are getting cynical! You'll have to

qualify that statement, Imogen.'

Imogen pulled up at traffic lights and turned to look at him.

'There's too much at stake for me to be totally happy, and in any case happiness is such a relative thing, and can be timed in seconds rather than hours or days.' The lights changed and she moved on.

'How true.' He regarded her through half closed eyes. 'Why is this particular play so important to you?'

The question was shot at her hard and for a moment she was at a loss for words. Recovering, she frowned, saying:

'Well, I . . . wouldn't like to let Adam down, he did cast me, after all . . . or the company, and it's my first play away from . . . my father. Of course it's important I do well.'

'For Gerard.'

'No. Yes. For him, of course. Naturally I want him to be proud of me. But it's important for me too, to show that I can work anywhere, not just for the Adair Company.' She flicked him a glance. 'Why are you looking at me like that?'

'Because I don't believe you. I think, more than anything, you want to please Gerard.'

'You can think what you damn well like!' she retorted, and swung into the theatre parking space. Nat's hand gripped her arm, restraining her from getting out.

'Have you told Gerard about me? No, I can tell by your face that you haven't. You've an expressive face, Imogen. Your thoughts are not mirrored quite so much as they used to be, but I can understand this particular topic being a fragile one. I don't blame you not telling him.'

'I have told him,' Imogen said coldly. 'At least, I

have the letter here for posting. You cast yourself with too much importance, Nat.'

'None of my doing, it's a role thrust on me, and I wish I had your confidence. Unfortunately, your dear daddy sees me as the devil incarnate. However, he's in America, out of harm's way, and . . .' his brows lifted '. . . perhaps you're not so firmly beneath his thumb as you used to be.'

'That's a lousy thing to say!'

'I'm willing to apologise when you prove me wrong. It's not completely your fault, Imogen. You've been too long conditioned to being a Daddy's girl.'

'Don't call me that!' Imogen ground out furiously.

There was a long silence. Sadie and her boy-friend were walking towards the stage door entrance, arm in arm, heads close. When they disappeared from sight, Nat drawled:

'You're right. Until you change your name from Beaumont you're my girl—whether we like it or not.' He heaved himself out awkwardly and strode into the theatre. Imogen sat on, her hands gripping the wheel, knuckles showing white.

For God's sake, how had all this erupted? she asked herself grimly. All because I said I wished he wouldn't smoke! A simple comment. She looked at her watch and moved quickly. If she was not careful, he would be bawling her out for being late.

The stage crew had worked that Sunday putting up the set and the Forest of Arden was beginning to grow before their eyes.

The technical rehearsal, dealing with sound effects and lighting, began after lunch. It was a disjointed affair so far as the actors were concerned, often demanding stopping and starting while the technical side was perfected.

Nat stalked about looking pale and drawn, making no allowances for his injury. Imogen handed over the pain-killers to Sadie and wished her luck. Towards the end of the rehearsal, when Nat had finished giving notes, she approached him to ask when he would like to be taken home.

He frowned down at her. 'I'll get someone else to do it. You go off now.'

Imogen hesitated, saying diffidently: 'What about tomorrow? Shall I . . .'

'Leave it—I'll organise something.'

'Very well.' Imogen turned away, relieved.

Dress rehearsal was called for six-thirty prompt. Imogen arrived at five, tracked down the leather waistcoat from Wardrobe that had needed to be altered, had a cup of tea and a chat with some of the cast in the theatre bar and then made for the dressing room. The redhead, Donna Campbell, drifted in and began to talk, but soon turned to someone else. For that, Imogen gave thanks. Loquacious females she could do without. She tried to analyse her feelings about the dress rehearsal. Certainly it was going to be good working in costume, that always helped to get you into character. She frowned slightly. There was a quick change from boy's clothes to wedding dress at the end, but Wardrobe were very efficient. She would have to make the change in the wings, no time to get to the dressing-room and back, so she must remember to ask Wardrobe to bring a mirror with them. She refused to allow herself to go over any of the speeches. She knew them, had been re-hearsing long enough to be confident in them. Now she only needed to clear her mind of everything and relax.

There were a couple of technical hitches during

the performance, but those apart, the play went well. Nat had made certain that there were a few invited members in the audience, which helped the cast, especially by their applause.

The bar was full of cast and crew members, talking and relaxing, and there was an air of controlled excitement and exuberance by the time Imogen arrived. She met Liz and Adam, who had been part of the audience, and her spirits rose as she received their sincere praise, both for the play as a whole and also for her own performance. She felt quietly confident now, knowing she had pulled it off, with Nat's help, and it was up to her to rise to those extra heights demanded of a critical first night audience. They were to have a final dress rehearsal tomorrow afternoon, and then it was to be the real thing, and despite her confidence, she found a shiver going down her spine at the thought.

'Here's your drink, Imogen,' said Drew, handing her a glass, which she took with a smile of thanks. 'Everyone seems to think it went well,' he went on, 'and the boss sounds satisfied. I must say he's a damned good director.' Drew took a drink, his eyes resting on Nat standing at the bar with Adam and Liz. Imogen murmured her agreement, thinking that Nat still seemed slightly haggard, but he did look pleased. His hand was out of the sling and Imogen wondered if that meant it was not so painful, or that Nat-like, he refused to pander to the sling's limitations. She rather thought it was the latter.

Nat said something that made Adam and Liz laugh. Imogen had been slightly worried about Liz now that she knew about herself and Nat. She hoped that she had not forced an imposition on to her friend, causing Liz any embarrassment when she was with Nat. Now, looking at her friend's animated face,

she realised that she need not have worried. Liz
could cope, and her instinct had been right. Liz had
known both Nat and herself for some time and would
be able to assess the situation knowing the background histories. Once or twice Imogen had felt the
urge to unburden herself to Sadie, but had resisted.
Only someone like Liz could fully understand the
complexities of the whole affair.

Imogen circulated, feeling happy and relaxed, and
a little later found Adam's arm drawing her into
their circle, as he said warmly:

'I've just been telling Nat what a lovely Rosalind
you are, Imogen, and he agrees, with me, that you
make a grand boy,' and Adam grinned.

Imogen's dimples appeared and her eyes gleamed
with amusement as she replied demurely: 'Thank
you. If I pass the Carlyon and Beaumont test, I'm
proud indeed!'

Adam cocked a quizzical brow at Nat. 'What do
you think she means by that, Beau?' and Nat replied
with mock hurt: 'I have no idea.'

'She means that you two know a good pair of legs
when you see them,' Liz quipped. 'Seriously, there's
something irresistible about a woman playing the
part of a man, isn't there? Audiences love it.' She
caught sight of Drew passing by and called to him:
'Andrew, my dear, I haven't seen you yet to con-
gratulate you on your Orlando. You and Imogen
make a lovely pair of lovers, and I must admit that
you make Orlando seem wonderfully plausible for a
change.'

Drew bowed his head in thanks, confiding: 'To
tell the truth, I find Orlando a pain in the neck and
therefore something of a challenge.'

They all laughed, Adam breaking in with: 'I know
what you mean. One feels he must be stupid not to

see through Rosalind's disguise. You do the only thing possible by making him so lovesick that he can't see the wood for the trees.'

Nat had been silent all this time and now asked the company in general: 'Do you think it's possible to be as lovesick as that?' His gaze passed round until it rested gently on Imogen, eyebrows raised.

Liz came in briskly with: 'Perfectly possible . . . after all, they do say love is blind.'

Adam smiled. 'There's a French proverb which says: Try to reason about love, and you will lose your reason.'

'I've been in love a hundred times,' Drew declared wickedly, 'but it's never made me sick yet.'

All eyes, it now seemed, were on Imogen, for her reply. She prevaricated with: 'Are you going to answer your own question?' to Nat, who merely gave an enigmatic smile. 'Very well, I too shall fall back on a quote, Dryden, I think it was, who said: "Heaven be thanked, we live in such an age, when no man dies for love, but on the stage".' She raised the glass to her lips, her eyes challenging Nat above the rim as the others laughed at the aptness of the quote.

'Come on, Nat, it's your turn,' declared Liz teasingly, and Nat said blandly: 'I refuse on the grounds that anything I may say will be . . .'

'Once a lawyer, always a lawyer,' groaned Adam, and Liz said:

'You disappoint me, Nat. I quite expected a really cynical quotation from you.'

Nat laughed and put his arm affectionately round Liz's shoulder. 'Dear Lizzie, I should hate to disappoint you.' He thought hard for a moment and, eyes gleaming with amusement, intoned: ' "If there's delight in love, 'tis when I see that heart which others bleed for, bleed for me".' He waited while the protests died down and added: 'Or better still—"There is only one way to be happy by means of the heart—to have none".'

'Well, I asked for it,' grumbled Liz goodnaturedly. 'I bet you could go on for hours like that.'

A little later, Liz took Imogen on one side. 'I know you don't want to be late and I can see Adam's been grabbed for an ear-bashing by one of the theatre Trustees, so I've left a message with Nat saying I've gone on home to relieve the baby-sitter. Will you come with me so I can run the sitter home? I don't like leaving the children, even for a quarter of an hour, on their own.'

Imogen drained her glass. 'Yes, of course. I'm ready to leave.' As they wended their way through the crush, she added: 'How will Adam get home?'

'He'll scrounge a lift from someone,' asserted Liz, and on the journey back to Treetops she chatted about the play and made a few pertinent comments.

On arrival, however, all thoughts of the play were banished at the sight of a pathetic Michael sitting forlorn on the sofa while a worried baby-sitter was hunting clean sheets for his bed. Liz immediately became calm and practical, making light of the sickness while she comforted Michael, apologising to the sitter who was only a young student and seemed in a bit of a flap. When Imogen offered to run the sitter home, Liz accepted with thanks.

On the way back from the student hostel, the BMW coughed, spluttered and came to a sudden halt. Imogen started the motor again, but it was dead. She sat there for a moment, frowning, her eyes passing over the dials. Oil, water, petrol—all seemed perfectly normal. She tried the engine again, to no avail. She looked at her watch, thought hard, and then got out, hurrying to a telephone box, some hundred yards farther down the road.

She dialled the theatre number, explained who she was, and what had happened, and asked for a message to be taken to Adam.

She walked slowly back to the BMW and tried the starter again, without much optimism, and once more looked at her watch. Nearly twelve o'clock, stranded in a dark, tree-lined road in the suburbs, with not a soul or a vehicle in sight, was not an ideal situation to be in. This was once a high-class residential area, but most of the large houses were now converted into flats, nursing homes or hostels and were set well back behind high walls or hedges. The BMW had stopped between two street lamps and although Imogen was not normally of a nervous disposition she found herself prickling with a certain amount of tension.

Another look at the watch made her decide to ring Liz, and when she opened the door and stepped out a voice said:

'What's the matter? Broken down?'

She swung round, giving a startled gasp, and a man in a trilby and raincoat was standing in the darker shadows beneath the trees. He stepped off the pavement and came round the car.

'Can I help?'

Imogen pulled herself together. 'That's very kind of you, but I'm expecting someone to come any minute now.'

'I saw you fifteen minutes ago. Thought, now what's a pretty young woman sitting there all alone for?'

'Yes, well, as I say, someone's coming . . .' Imogen strove to keep her voice calm and friendly—not too friendly, more polite. 'It's kind of you, but there's no need for you to bother.'

'Oh, no bother. It'd be a pleasure to help a lady in distress.'

Imogen's heart sank. He looked respectable enough, but was his voice a little too knowing? his smile more of a leer? Or was her overworked imagination succumbing to the panic welling up inside? A casual look either way brought no help.

'Now then, where's the catch for the bonnet?' He came nearer and Imogen said more firmly:

'Really, there's no need. The car isn't mine and the owner will be coming along. I don't think . . .'

'Oh? The car's not yours, then? Just borrowed it, have you?'

'Yes.' Imogen closed the door with a slam and locked it. 'Thank you for your offer of help, but . . .' She began walking towards the kiosk. It seemed miles away. She had given him a polite smile as she had swung off and her heart was hammering away so much that she could not make out whether he was following or not. At last the kiosk was reached and irrationally she felt more secure in its well-lit shelter. She dialled Treetops and found the line engaged.

Imogen bit her lip, her eyes searching the road. Oh, for the sight of a good old-fashioned bobby on the beat! The man was standing by the car, looking this way. Was she being silly? Imaginative? She pressed down the bar and dialled again, her eyes fixed on the BMW. He was still there, waiting, and the line continued to be engaged.

Where, oh, where was Adam?

A set of headlights came round the bottom corner, travelling slowly. She held her breath. It was a taxi. She thrust the receiver down on to its hook and pushed open the door, thinking that she would stop that taxi even if she had to throw herself under its wheels.

The taxi stopped beyond the BMW and a figure stepped out. The vehicle did a three-point turn and went off the way it had come. Disappointment and frustration welled up in Imogen's throat and her steps faltered. The passenger began to cross the road towards her and called her name and she rushed forward, crying: 'Adam!' and threw herself into his arms.

Instantly, intuitively, she knew it was Nat. Cursing the dimly lit road, she thrust herself away, noting vaguely that his arms had only made a token gesture of comfort.

'What's the matter?' Nat asked abruptly, peering through the darkness to see her face.

'Nothing ... I ...' She turned away, her eyes seeking the man, but they seemed alone. She fumbled for the car keys in her pocket and as she led him to the BMW, face averted, said brightly: 'Am I glad to see you! Don't ask me what's wrong with the blessed car because engines are an unknown quantity. I just get in and expect them to run.' Even to her ears she sounded peculiar. 'It went perfectly and then petered out.' She thought her face ought to be reasonable now and lifted her head from the interior after inserting the ignition key. Nat was standing closer than she realised. 'It's all yours,' she added, and went to move away.

He took her arm, restraining her. 'Why are you trembling?'

To her everlasting shame Imogen burst into tears, turning away, her hands coming up to hide her face. Giving a muttered exclamation, Nat turned her round and pulled her to him, his arms holding her close. For a few seconds Imogen allowed herself the comfort of his chest and then giving a hiccuping sob that tried to be a laugh, made a movement away and his arms loosened their hold. He held out a handkerchief which she took gratefully.

'I'm sorry.' She mopped up, mortified with her ourburst, and Nat said briefly:

'Get in the other side and wait while I try and sort this out.'

With mixed feelings Imogen did as she was told while Nat busied himself under the bonnet. In a ridiculously short time he slid behind the wheel and tried the engine. It leapt to life.

'That's it . . . a loose connection on the ignition, a simple job if you know what to look for.' He regarded her consideringly and then said gently: 'Have you finished with the hanky?' Imogen nodded and he took it, wiping his hands as he got out to put down the bonnet. When he returned he made no move to start the engine again and said: 'What's happened to upset you?' He saw her hesitate and went on firmly: 'Tell me.'

She gave a self-derisive shrug and related all that had happened, finishing up wryly: 'I probably let my imagination run completely away with me. He could have been legitimately eager to help with no evil designs. Looking back now I can't imagaine how I became so panicky.'

'Why the hell didn't you bring Poss, or do you only bring him along for protection against me?'

'He was out on the prowl, and in any case, I didn't think.'

Nat was silent for a moment. 'It doesn't matter what his intentions were, the situation was not a desirable one. I would have been happier had you just locked yourself in the car and sat it out.'

'I would have if I'd known that my message had actually reached Adam.' She paused and said lightly: 'I'm sorry you had to come and rescue me and then suffer near-hysterics. I'm not usually so frenetic.'

'Think nothing of it.' Nat started the engine and moved away from the kerb.

Imogen gave an inward sigh. Forget it. That would, no doubt, be easy, all except those first few seconds when his arms closed so reluctantly round her.

'I suppose Adam had already left for home?' she suggested, and Nat's 'Yes,' seemed to indicate that he was not in the mood for talk.

When he swung into the drive at Treetops she said hesitantly:

'You should have gone to your flat first, I could easily have driven myself on from there. What shall you do now?'

Nat half turned in his seat and answered a laconic: 'Walk.'

'At this hour? How ridiculous, Nat! You look tired and not well. Please let me ring for a taxi?' She gave an exasperated sigh. 'I know there's no point in offering you the Rover.'

'None.'

'Which is childish. Just because it's Gerard's!'

'Exactly.' He gave an ugly twist to his lips and said harshly: 'It would be just my luck to smash it up—and think what a field day Gerard would have then.'

'It pleases you to say things like that,' she said quietly. 'Will you take the BMW? Adam would . . .'

'I shall walk.'

The tone was not to be argued with further. He opened his door and got out, Imogen following suit. There was little light from the night sky and she was grateful for Nat's grip on her arm. She halted on the step, the front door key in her hand. Not one to give up easily, she murmured softly:

'You won't let me ring for a taxi?' She saw him shake his head and went on crossly: 'You really are pigheaded, Nat. Well, goodnight. Thank you for coming. I'm sorry to have been such a nuisance.' She gave a soft laugh. 'I never was so glad to see anyone in my whole life!'

'Really? I thought it was Adam you wanted, the way you flung yourself into my arms. Sorry to have disappointed you,' Nat concluded silkily.

Imogen stood still, her emotions changing from puzzlement, understanding and anger with alarming rapidity.

'Just what do you mean by that, Nathaniel Beaumont?' she demanded quietly.

'Do I have to spell it out? Has Adam undertaken the father-figure while Gerard's in America? Or is he to step into my shoes?'

'Damn you, Nat . . .'

'Just don't forget that Adam's only cut out to be his own kids' father-figure—he's a mite too young to be yours. I'll not have Lizzie hurt through your inadequacies.' He backed off the step. 'Goodnight.'

Dully Imogen watched his dark shape disappear down the drive.

Well, that was really that. In two seconds flat Nat had destroyed the easy and affectionate relationship she had with both Adam and Liz. In one fell swoop he had cut the ground from beneath her. She opened the door. God! If, for one moment, she thought that either of them believed that she . . .!

As she crept silently to her room she knew that she could no longer remain here. Tomorrow she would look for somewhere to live.

CHAPTER SEVEN

'It was a lover and his lass'

'BUT why?' asked Liz in bewilderment. 'Aren't you happy staying here with us?'

'Of course I am, silly, but honestly, Lizzie, I never intended staying with you for the whole of the time, you know that. The days have just gone by without me realising it. Adam will be going to Paris tomorrow and I know he wants you to spend part of the time with him over there . . .'

'Yes, he does, but I thought you could invite Sadie over to stay with you while . . .'

'It will be much better if you shut the house up totally. It would be far too much of a responsibility for me.'

This silenced Liz, as Imogen hoped it would.

Liz sighed. 'If you're positive. Adam will be surprised. He had hoped . . .'

'Adam knows, as you do, that it will be a nice change to have somewhere of my own.' Imogen lowered her lids, avoiding her friend's eyes, hoping she would take the hint. Liz, bless her, did, and grinned.

'I suppose we do rather cramp your style. Okay, I give in. Have you found somewhere?'

'Yes,' lied Imogen, 'but you can't visit until I've got it ship-shape. How's Michael this morning?'

'Seems fine. You know what kids are, up one minute, down the next.'

'I'm glad.' Imogen pushed back her chair and

rose. 'By the way, I had trouble with the BMW last
night on the way back from dropping off the sitter. I
phoned the theatre and Nat came and put it right,
only took him a second or two.' She hastily drank
the remains of her tea. 'Must dash now. See you
later.'

Imogen was lucky to find a room in the same row
of houses as Sadie's. She had gone straight to Sadie's
lodgings and after her friend's initial surprise they
had hunted round, making enquiries, resulting in a
small, but adequate, room two doors down.

Imogen could not believe her luck. The room had
a window that overlooked a small conservatory built
on to the back of the house. She checked with the
landlord and received permission to bring Poss with
her, and then explained her enthusiasm to Sadie.

'When I go out I shall be able to leave the window
open at the bottom and Poss can come in and out
when he pleases.'

'Share kitchen, bathroom and the draught under
the door,' Sadie joked, looking round the room criti-
cally. 'As places go, it's not so bad, and you'll find it
convenient for the theatre.' She straightened a
cracked mirror. 'Not up to Treetops' standard, I'm
afraid.'

Imogen moved to the window and gazed out on
to a row of small back gardens, utility sheds and the
backs of a similar row of houses.

'I didn't expect it to be.' She turned and smiled.
'Don't worry, Sadie. I've been in worse places, believe me.'

Relief showed on her friend's face. 'The thing is,
Imogen, you look as if you've been used to nothing
but the best. I thought you'd turn tail and run!' She
sat on the bed and tested it, pulling a comical face.
'If you're determined to move in today, shall I

borrow Doug's car and help you? We can go to the super-store and get some groceries, then on to fetch Poss and your cases.'

'Sadie, you're an angel!' exclaimed Imogen, and almost pushed her friend out of the room.

Poss was philosophical. He sniffed round the room, prowled round the garden and accepted that the window was to be his freedom gate.

'When you've got used to the neighbourhood you can go out on your own, but for now I'm closing the window.' Imogen gave him some fuss and then kissed the top of his head. 'Wish me luck! I'll come back in between dress rehearsal and curtain up, so you won't be left for long on your own.'

She timed herself walking to the theatre and found that it took fifteen minutes at an easy pace. Coming home late, she would either catch a bus, or cadge a lift from Sadie and Doug.

She hardly gave the blue Mercedes a glance as she walked by, but brief though it was she noticed it looked good as new. Inside the theatre everyone seemed purposeful and efficient. There were television cameras set up in the auditorium and Jake Edwards smiled as she went past, suddenly calling her name. She turned, eyeing him curiously, and he came up to her, his face friendly, saying:

'Do you mind if I ask you something?' and when Imogen shook her head, wondering what was coming, he went on: 'Do you realise that you have an ideal camera face?'

She showed her surprise in face and voice. 'I have? Really?'

He nodded. 'Have you ever thought of doing any work?' Someone shouted across the auditorium and he waved a 'just a minute' hand, digging into his pocket and bringing out a card. 'Look, here's a

number that can reach me if you're interested. And
if you can, try and catch this profile on Beau
Beaumont. You'll see what I mean.' He grinned and
handed her the card. 'I'm not selling you a line.
Beau agrees with me. Saw the early takes,' and with
a cheery nod he left her and went back to his crew.

In rather a daze Imogen slipped the card into her
bag and made for the dressing room, soon forgetting
Jake's surprising announcement in the preparation
for changing herself into Rosalind.

As a 'final dress' it went well. Nat called the cast
on stage for notes, although there were only a few.
When he came to the final one he screwed the sheet
of paper into a ball in a symbolic gesture and aimed
it at Sadie, who caught it expertly.

'Right, that's it. Up to you now.' Nat looked
round the assembled company and smiled encouragingly. 'Thank you for your co-operation, your enthusiasm and hard work. It will have paid off, you'll
see. We have a good show here and I've no worries.
Go away now and relax . . . and be ready for curtain
up at seven-thirty.'

On the way home to their lodgings in Sycamore
Terrace—a misnomer if you liked, snorted Sadie on
showing Imogen around, with not a tree in sight—
Sadie said dryly:

'If Nathaniel Beaumont said go on a slow boat to
China we'd all go.'

They were sitting in the back seat of Doug's Mini
and Imogen asked teasingly:

'Does Doug approve of this hero-worship?' and
watched Sadie's boy-friend grin through the rear-
view mirror.

'Oh, they're just as bad in the lighting box. Think
he's a bloomin' marvel, they do, don't you, Doug?
What the Beau doesn't know about lighting could

be put on a postage stamp,' declared Sadie airily. When Doug stopped the car to let the girls out they made arrangements for the return journey and went their separate ways.

Imogen had time for an hour's rest, forced herself to eat a poached egg on toast and after sorting Poss out, was down on the pavement waiting for the Mini at six-thirty.

There was a telegram from Gerard waiting for her, sending her his love and best wishes for the first night. Imogen stuck it on the dressing room mirror near to where she was sitting and Donna said:

'Is Gerard Adair your father? I didn't realise that. He's sent a cable to the whole Company too, did you know? It's on the notice-board outside. Rather sweet of him. What's he doing in America?'

Imogen told her while they made up, and smiled to herself that Donna should find her worth talking to now that she was Gerard Adair's daughter.

'Is he coming to see the play?' Donna asked, adjusting the lace on her dress and admiring herself in the mirror.

'Yes, he'll make the last performance,' replied Imogen, her thoughts suddenly flying to the letter, waiting for him at Washington, telling him about Nat.

'Fifteen minutes, please.' Sadie's voice came over the tannoy and everyone began to panic, with ejaculations of 'Fifteen minutes, is that all!' or 'Did she say fifteen minutes? Surely not!'

Imogen did not allow herself to be panicked. She had learned from her father the benefits of allowing enough time before going on to a stage. She was dressed and made up and all she had to do was to think about Rosalind, who was banished from court and had to seek refuge in the Forest of Arden clothed as a youth.

Nat walked in to the dressing-room, relaxed and confident, making teasing jokes as he made his way round the room. Imogen slipped into the cloakroom and waited until she heard him go. It was childish of her, but if he could be childish, so could she.

'Five minutes. Beginners for act one, please. Orlando, Adam, Oliver, Charles . . .'

'Good luck, everybody,' 'the same to you,' echoed round the dressing-rooms and waiting area.

'One minute to curtain. One minute. House lights going down, begin the music . . .'

Imogen hesitated at the mirror. Rosalind made a pretty girl, too, she decided, although her glance went to the cream silk blouse with the full sleeves and the soft suede three-quarter trousers with matching waistcoat, hanging ready on a coathanger for her transformation into a boy. A movement in the open doorway caught her eye and Nat came into view. Imogen had known she would not be able to keep out of his way completely. She did not move or speak, merely held his look through the mirror.

Nat came forward a few steps. 'You disappeared. Intentionally?' He leaned indolently against the rack of costumes, curving his right arm round the end hook. 'If you're spoiling for a fight prior to your first night entrance, you'd better think again, Imogen,' he told her softly.

Imogen lifted one shoulder a trifle disdainfully and smiled. She was quite pleased with that smile when she thought about it afterwards.

'I'm not spoiling for a fight, Nat. You've done your job and now I'm going to do mine. You've never really understood me, have you? You've always thought me weak—goodness knows why you bothered with me in the first place. Well, I might be weak in some areas, but not where my job is concerned. I shall go on tonight and give the performance you want from me, whether we have a fight or not. I don't collapse so easy.' She broke the gaze and absently dropped some sticks of make-up into her box, tossing a used piece of cotton wool into the waste bin.

'I see.' Nat left the rack and hitched himself against the back of a chair, folding his arms across his chest. Imogen studiously ignored him, but she could not ignore the image he left in her mind's eye. He was wearing a suit for this important first night, although now he only sported the waistcoat, and the cream shirt was tie-less and open at the neck, the sleeves rolled up to the elbows. It looked a very expensive suit, Imogen considered, and the light brown colour suited him. His shoes, which he was so casually studying at the moment, were soft tan leather. Altogether a 'costly dish', as Sadie would say. And when he had made himself presentable for the usual drinks with the Trustees and civic dignitaries who were out front tonight, when the tie was tied and the sleeves rolled down, jacket donned, why, then Sadie would say, what an 'attractive dish!'

'So you don't want me to wish you luck?' His voice was a drawl.

'You can if you like. I don't really think luck comes into it much. I'd rather cling to all the hard work you've put into both my role and the production, which is more concrete than luck.'

'So you do give me the credit for something?'

She turned to him now. 'Why, of course. I have a tremendous admiration for your work, Nat. Surely you must know that? Any success we achieve tonight will be mostly yours,' and her voice was strongly sincere, and she did not waver as she met his coolly deliberate look.

'Humm . . . Liz tells me you've moved.' He waited a moment for some reaction and when there was none, went on: 'She was rather upset at the abruptness of your decision to go.'

'Oh, I don't think so,' Imogen said easily. 'She knew it was going to happen eventually.'

'Where are you living now?'

Imogen said simply: 'I can't think of any reason, Nat, why I should tell you.'

'I see.' He hoisted himself to his feet, gave a fleeting glance at the telegram from Gerard stuck to the mirror and said pleasantly: 'Whether you want me to or not, I'm going to wish you luck, my love. There is that infinitesimal something, a hint of theatrical superstition that I'm loath to admit to, but which is there, nonetheless.' He gave his slow smile. 'So . . . good luck, Imogen. You deserve it,' and putting fingertips to lips he blew her a tantalising kiss before sauntering out.

Imogen expelled a long breath. She felt as though she had just run a long race and didn't know if she had won. She rather thought it was a dead heat.

Sadie bustled in, carrying a drink, looking back over her shoulder before eyeing Imogen shrewdly. 'Here, a present from Dougie.'

'Sadie, how sweet of him! If you get a chance, tell him he's a dear.'

'Okay.' Sadie eyed her speculatively. 'What was our gorgeous director doing in the ladies' room?'

'Merely wishing me good luck,' Imogen said calmly, 'and there's my cue call. I must go,' and she hurried out, conscious of Sadie grinning and saying: 'How nice of him,' as she followed.

Perhaps Nat's good luck wishes helped after all.

Waiting in the wings to go on, Imogen found herself
tingling with anticipation rather than actual nerves.
Whether she would admit it to herself or not, Nat's
'you deserve it' meant a lot. Sadie grinned and gave
the thumbs-up sign and then Imogen was following
Donna on stage, and Donna's Celia was saying: 'I
pray thee, Rosalind, sweet my coz, be merry,' and
Imogen was replying, confidently and just how Nat
wanted her to.

The after-show party in the bar was going a bomb.
The members of the Company were finding it possible to eat, drink and be merry, for the audience
reaction was extremely gratifying. Everyone agreed
that they had a success on their hands.

Imogen was with Drew, quite content to stand by
his side, his arm round her shoulder, while she drank
the wine and ate the delicious assortment of savouries
provided. She was feeling satiated with a sense of
achievement, of which Drew was an essential part.
Their Rosalind and Orlando tonight had reached
some delightful delicate heights and she was feeling
warmly grateful to Drew for being such a good foil.

Nat was standing at the far side of the bar, talking
to Jake Edwards, and Donna was part of the group.
Now he was listening to Jake and his eyes came to
rest on Imogen, leaning comfortably back against
Drew. She lifted her glass in a silent toast and after a
moment, long enough for Imogen to think he was
going to ignore it, he returned the salute. It was
difficult to know what he was thinking, Imogen
decided, while she gained some private amusement
in the fact that now he had ousted her from Treetops
she was beyond his reach.

When Drew asked if she wanted a lift home she
accepted and was aware of both Sadie's and Nat's
eyes on them as they left the theatre. On the way,

Drew asked: 'Tired?' and she nodded, closing her eyes and leaning her head back against the seat. When he turned into Sycamore Terrace he pulled up outside the house Imogen indicated and turned to look at her, saying:

'Here we are—are you going to invite me up?' and his glance was teasing.

'The landlord does not appreciate gentlemen callers,' she replied primly, and then smiled. 'Not tonight, Drew. Thank you for the lift, and for being such a rock on stage tonight. You were wonderful.'

Drew returned her smile. 'How about showing your gratitude in the usual manner?' he asked, and Imogen leaned forward and placed her lips against his.

'Mmm ... very nice,' responded Drew appreciatively. He sat back and looked at her intently. 'You know, Imogen, you're a bit of an enigma, did you know that?' She shook her head. 'I admit your old man scared the living daylights out of me when I worked for him, but even now you have that "touch me not" aura about you and he's not around. Am I right in suspecting that someone has beat me to it?' he asked quizzically.

Imogen smiled ruefully and nodded her head. 'Something like that,' she admitted quietly. 'It's not all that straightforward.'

'No need to explain, poppet. Out you get and have your full quota of beauty sleep—we've a long run ahead of us.'

Imogen kissed him quickly on the cheek and scrambled out. Before closing the door she whispered: 'You're a pal, Drew.'

'Yes, I know,' he remarked dryly, and giving a farewell wave, drove off.

Life fitted into a routine. Adam left for France

and now that her days were her own Imogen spent some of them with Liz, who was missing him. Imogen hardly saw Nat, who was rehearsing the next play during the day, usually wandering in most nights, sometimes briefly, sometimes for the whole performance, but contact with her was only in a group.

She received a couple of letters from Gerard and another from Duggan. Things seemed to be going well in America. She had not sent on the reviews of *As You Like It* because Nat's name was mentioned. Better to show Pa those herself, Imogen considered. The reviews were good, and it pleased her to see her name and Nat's within the same paragraph.

She still went round with Drew, sometimes making a foursome with Sadie and Doug. They once saw an attractive, dark-haired girl getting into the Mercedes outside the theatre and Sadie whispered: 'The solicitor woman!' and Imogen nodded and wished she could fall in love with Drew.

At the beginning of the final week of the run, Liz flew to Paris with the children intending to stay with Adam for about ten days. Imogen was rather lonely during the day now, for Sadie and Doug were working and she did not want to encourage Drew, or use him.

On the last Friday, Poss went missing. Imogen did not worry too much at first, but when he did not return for his evening meal she went out to look for him. She questioned the other residents but no one had seen anything of him all day, so she left the window open and his food available and reluctantly took herself off to the theatre.

When the play finished Imogen slipped away early, not feeling like staying behind for a chat in the bar. When she reached the bus stop one was just sailing away in the distance, and swallowing her annoyance she prepared to wait for the next. It was chilly, even though it was early May, and she zipped up her jacket and dug her hands into her pockets.

The blue Mercedes drew up at the kerb and Nat reached across and pushed open the passenger door.

'Can I take you anywhere, lady?'

Imogen hesitated briefly and then got in and Nat waited while she fixed the seat belt before driving on. Presently she said:

'For someone who doesn't know the way, you seem . . .' and then stopped. Sycamore Terrace was not to be their destination, it seemed.

'We have to talk, Imogen.'

'Do we?'

'Yes. Gerard comes home tomorrow and tonight is our last chance.'

Imogen made no reply. Maybe it was. Nat drew into the courtyard of his block of flats and they went in, in silence.

'Drink?' queried Nat, and Imogen nodded, watching him mix a Martini, the way he knew she liked it. When his own glass was filled, Nat raised it mockingly, and murmured: 'Here's to us.'

Imogen raised hers and said quietly: 'I'd rather drink to the future.'

'By all means.' He deliberated for a few moments. 'To us, and the future.' They drank, and because the tension was rising dangerously between them, Imogen allowed her eyes to go idly round the room, arrested by a picture she had not noticed before. She walked over and stood gazing at the watercolour, saying:

'You take it round with you?'

'Makes the place feel like home.' Nat came to stand behind her. 'Does it bring back memories?'

It seemed too real, somehow—the long stretch of beach with the grey sea and white-capped waves. You could tell that the wind was blowing, for the marram grass was bent over in the dunes and the sand was lifting. A solitary walker was in the distance, and a dog was investigating something at the waterline.

There was a constriction in her throat and she took a drink, her voice unsteady as she asked:

'Is Lulu still as high-spirited as she used to be?'

There was amusement in Nat's voice as he remarked: 'Not quite. I have managed to get some sense into her over the past three years.'

'How much easier when it's only a dumb animal,' Imogen said, suddenly feeling exhausted. 'Human beings are more difficult, aren't they?' She heard the ice rattle in his glass as he took a drink before his hand reached out to take her glass and both were placed carefully on the table. As he turned her round to face him, she gabbled:

'I thought we were going to talk.'

'There's a time for talking—and I've decided that this isn't it.' Nat was stroking her hair and she began to tremble.

'Nat, I . . .'

'No talking, remember?' His lips, gentle and persuasive, halted any more breathless words. His hands left her hair and came down, cupping her face, and his lips were touching hers, again and again, each time for only the lightest of contact. His thumbs stroked her cheeks and then his lips claimed hers strongly and fiercely and he felt her body shudder and relax against him in surrender.

In one movement Nat swept her into his arms and carried her through to the bedroom, kicking the door so that it shut behind him. He laid her gently down on the bed, his eyes holding hers, their message strong and compelling, brilliant in their intensity, yet the overall expression on his face was guarded and his mouth was a little grim.

For a long moment he waited, giving her time to deny, to rebuff, before laying his head on her breast.

There was still time, Imogen told herself, to run, to fight, to reject.

Her hand came up and touched the back of his head, her fingers threading through the thick springiness of hair in his nape, following a downward path until her palm rested gently in the hollow of his shoulder blade. She felt him tense at the first sensation of her touch, his whole body motionless, poised as if he could hardly dare believe his own body sense. And then his head came up, his weight lifting from her, and his mouth claimed hers, hard and insistent, withdrawing abruptly to trace a line along the curve of her jaw, down her neck, his cheek coming to rest against the smoothness of her skin as he breathed in the faint, subtle perfume of her body.

An anguished groan escaped his lips and Nat almost snarled:

'God, Imogen, do you know what you do to me?' and she found laughter welling up inside, erupting and exploding into a mixture of power, desire, even pity for this man kneeling by her side. She murmured: 'Hush' and smoothed back the hair falling across his forehead, then urgency overcame them both, fingers wrestled impatiently with buttons and belts until flesh touched flesh, and life was once more consummate and complete.

Coming up out of the depths of sleep they touched, relearned, urgency gone and in its place gentleness and tenderness and the feeling that time had no meaning and that this moment was forever.

Waking, the early morning sunshine on her face through the uncurtained window, Imogen turned her head to gaze at Nat, still asleep. He was lying on his back, his head towards her. He was taking up three-quarters of the bed space and only a quarter of the covers lay across his long length. His chest rose rhythmically, the golden hair darkened with sweat. The hair lying across his forehead was also limp and moist and Imogen felt a rush of love sweeping over her as he gaze searched his face hungrily and she had to resist the temptation to place her lips against the vulnerable lines of his mouth.

For a little while she lay quietly, wallowing in the languor of her body and the feel of Nat's weight against her, before gathering together her strength of mind. Very, very gently she eased herself from the mattress, waiting a few anxious seconds in case he stirred and woke. Committed, she soft-footed across the carpet, picking up her clothes where they had been flung the night before, a smile teasing her lips as she did so. Opening the door carefully Imogen paused, her eyes taking their fill of the recumbent figure lying so peacefully on the bed, imagining him waking and finding her gone, and almost she was persuaded to return, so painful was it to leave him.

No. She had to go. The time to return to Nat for good was not now, not when Gerard was still away, and in his heart of hearts Nat must realise that too. She stifled a sigh and closed the door softly behind her. She dressed quickly and was out of the flat within ten minutes. Walking quickly along the almost deserted streets, for it was a mere six-thirty and not many people were abroad, she saw the first bus of the day and, running, managed to catch it by the skin of her teeth.

As soon as she let herself into her room Imogen knew that Poss had not returned and her happiness deserted her. She crossed to the window, taking in the untouched food and milk, knowing something had happened to him.

When the man came, carrying the piece of sacking, she was expecting him.

He lived, he told her, three doors down, and understood she had lost a cat. He was sorry if this one was hers. He thought it had been poisoned and apologetically lifted the sacking away.

When Imogen rang Sadie and explained, Sadie came at once in Doug's car and together they went over to Treetops. Imogen found a pleasant spot under a lilac tree and Sadie took herself off, scared that her own emotion would offend her friend, who was showing none. She sat in Doug's car and waited. After a while Imogen returned and climbed in. She merely said:

'I don't think Liz and Adam will mind, do you?' and Sadie answered: 'I'm sure they won't.'

On the way into the theatre that afternoon for the matinée performance, Sadie was relieved to find Imogen had lost much of the bleak look of the morning and they chatted, mostly about Gerard's arrival.

'Where's he staying?' Sadie asked, adding with a grin: 'I don't suppose he'd appreciate Sycamore Terrace.'

'I've booked him in at the Grand.' Imogen gave a nervous smile. 'I do hope he'll like the play.'

'Why shouldn't he? We got rave reviews. He's going to be really proud of you, Imogen. I heard our gorgeous director singing your praises the other night to some colleagues who'd come from London to see it.'

'Oh?' said Imogen, a warm glow spreading over her.

'Yes. Oh!' mimicked Sadie.

There was barely an hour's break between matinée and evening performance. Imogen changed into blouse and trousers and made her way to the telephone in the foyer and dialled the Grand, asking for her father's room. The girl on the switchboard told her there was no reply and, frowning, Imogen told her she would ring again.

'Really, Pa, can't you be on time just this once?' she muttered under her breath, and went to get a sandwich and coffee. She saw Nat sitting with some of the cast at another table and after a few minutes he excused himself and came over to her.

Imogen was very conscious of his regard from the other side of the table.

'Why did you go?' he asked, and Imogen took a sip of coffee before answering.

'You didn't really expect me to stay, did you, Nat? Last night was, perhaps, necessary for both of us, but it doesn't solve anything, does it?' She raised her brows questioningly and saw his jaw tighten.

'Imogen, Sadie has told me about Poss . . .' and Imogen broke in firmly: 'I don't want to talk about him.' She took another drink, lashes down, hiding her eyes.

'I understand.' Nat's face smoothed out into a courteously noncommittal mask. 'Has Gerard arrived yet?' and when Imogen shook her head, he persisted: 'He is due to come and see the play tonight, isn't he?'

'Yes. I've just rung the hotel, but they haven't arrived yet. Probably been held up somewhere. I've left the tickets at the box office.'

'Duggan will be with him, I suppose?'

Imogen said smilingly: 'Oh, yes, the faithful Duggan will be with him.' She stood up. 'Will you excuse me, Nat, while I phone again?'

This time, when she got through, the receptionist said quickly:

'Miss Adair, we have a telegram for you here. What should we do with it?'

Imogen gave a resigned sigh. 'Can you open it for me, please?'

'I'm sorry, we're not allowed to do that,' the girl's apologetic voice came down the line.

Imogen stifled her exasperation, looked at her watch and asked to speak to the manager. When he introduced himself, she explained urgently:

'Look, I know it's not hotel policy, but I'm expecting my father—who perhaps you know is Gerard Adair, the actor—to check in at the hotel and it's obvious he's been held up. I'm due on stage at the Queen's in about half an hour and no way am I going to be able to get to the hotel, pick up the telegram and be back here at the theatre in time.'

There was silence for a moment and the manager said:

'I understand, Miss Adair. May I say how much I enjoyed the play, and especially your performance the other evening?'

Imogen murmured: 'Thank you. I'm pleased you enjoyed it.' She heard paper crackling.

'Miss Adair? I cannot read this telegram to you over the telephone. I'm sorry.' His voice was greatly distressed. 'I'm sorry. I really don't know what to do for the best. Is there someone in authority I could speak with?'

Imogen stood quietly, the blood draining from her body.

'Miss Adair? Miss Adair, did you hear me? Are you still there?'

Through stiff lips, Imogen said: 'Yes, I'm still here.' She turned her head slowly as if it had suddenly become an immense weight. What was it the man had said? Someone in authority? Nat was standing watching her. She held the receiver out to him and said in a flat voice: 'He wants to talk to you.' Nat came close and took it, giving her a sharp look.

Imogen wandered over to the window and looked down on the city. Saturday evening and a steady flow of people making their way along the busy street, all knowing where they were going. Imogen thought how lucky they were, for suddenly she did not know where she was going any more.

The low murmur of Nat's voice in the background stopped and when she turned he was looking at her, his face angry. What has Nat to be so angry about? she found herself wondering. She allowed him to seat her in the reception office, listening without interruption.

'We have no details. Only that there has been an accident in America—a fatal one. Will you be all right if I leave you for a moment?'

She nodded. Of course she would be all right. What did he think she was going to do—run away? In a few minutes he returned with a wide-eyed, ashen-faced Sadie, who sat down by her side and took one of her hands between her own. Imogen smiled reassuringly. Nat, still looking grim, handed Imogen a glass and told her to drink it. She had never liked brandy and he knew that, but because he was looking so stern she drank it.

'What about tonight, Imogen? Do you still want to go on?'

She looked at him in surprise. 'Of course.' She

looked at her watch, hardly able to believe that only fifteen minutes had elapsed since she had so innocently dialled the hotel. She handed back the empty glass, saying: 'Thank you, Nat,' and not able to look at his face she walked out of the office, saying over her shoulder: 'Come on, Sadie, you'll be late.'

The news must have flown round the theatre like a bush fire. The dressing-room was strangely subdued and she could feel the glances turned her way. Imogen wished she could say: be natural, it's the last night, have fun—Pa would have wanted that . . . but she could only hope that her own calmness would ease the atmosphere.

The Saturday evening audience were out to be pleased and entertained, and the applause was loud after each act. Another brandy appeared, together with a chicken sandwich, and Imogen forced both down and was glad to hear the dressing-room getting more like itself. Before the last act Drew came in and kissed her forehead, tucking her arm companionably into his as they made for the wings. Of Nat there had been no sign, and she was glad.

The final curtain came down to tumultuous applause. Drew's hand squeezed hers tight and for one bewildering moment all the cast turned in her direction and stepped back a pace, leaving her on her own, which nearly proved her undoing, and then the curtain came down for the last time and Drew smiled at her and she smiled back and let him take her to the dressing-room where Sadie was waiting.

'Can I help you pack up, Imogen?' Sadie asked, her eyes anxious, and Imogen answered: 'Aren't you supposed to be helping strike the set?'

'I've been let off.' Sadie began to help whether Imogen wanted her to or not, so Imogen let her. When they had nearly finished, Imogen ventured:

'Has Nat found out anything more?' and Sadie shook
her head.

'There, I think that's all.' Imogen looked at her
friend and smiled rather wanly. 'You are a love.
Thank you, Sadie.'

'I'll fetch Nat, shall I?'

Imogen frowned. 'Why?'

Sadie stared at her uncertainly. 'Well . . . he . . . I
think he wants to take . . . care of you.'

'Does he?' Imogen thought for a moment. 'Sadie,
will you do something for me? Will you go and fetch
Drew?'

Sadie blinked. 'Drew?' She looked disappointed.
'You want me to fetch Drew?'

'Yes.' Imogen looked absently round the empty
dressing room and then brought her attention back
to the worried Sadie. 'Look, Sadie, be my good
friend. I promise you that I'm not doing anything
silly. I just want you to fetch Drew and then go and
pretty yourself up for Doug and the party. I'm all
right, honestly.'

Sadie gave her a long look, must have been reassured, and went.

The 'good luck' cards were still stuck to the
mirror. Imogen took them all down and tossed them
into the waste-bin, keeping the telegram from
Gerard, folding it and putting it carefully in her bag.
She looked up as Drew entered, saying quickly:

'Drew, will you do something for me?'

'Of course.' Drew smiled, kindly concern on his
face. Much, much better than that other, angry face.

'Will you take me back to my room and on to the
Grand Hotel?'

'If that's what you want.'

'It is. And when you've done that I want you to
come back here to the party.' She gazed at him

calmly and he gave an assenting nod of the head. As
they got into his car, Drew remarked:

'Is Nat Beaumont going to like this, Imogen?' and
she replied:

'I don't think so.'

The hotel room was bare but adequate and when
the manager left them, his expression unhappy, they
stood for a moment in silence until Imogen said
firmly:

'I shall be all right, Drew,' and he pulled his
mouth down at the corners and took her in his arms,
giving her a gentle hug.

'Yes.' He pulled out a diary and ripped a page
from the centre on which he quickly wrote a number.
'This will find me. If you want me, I'll come.'

'Thank you, Drew, you are a dear,' Imogen whispered, and at last she was alone. Still calm, still
competent, she rang down to reception saying that
she did not wish to take any calls until the morning
and took herself off to bed. She dozed, on and off,
finally falling into a deep sleep at the time she would
normally be waking. The ringing of the telephone
woke her and, muddle-headed, she answered it.

'Imogen? Drew here. Look, love, I expect you
knew that Nat would eventually buttonhole me.
Sorry, but he'll be round to you shortly . . . I couldn't
hold him off.'

'Thanks, Drew. I hope he didn't give you a black
eye?' Imogen asked anxiously, and heard him laugh.

'No, but very nearly. Would you like me to come
round?'

'Thanks, but that won't be necessary.'

'Well, I only hope you know what you're doing,
Imogen. He's a very determined customer, our Mr
Beaumont.'

'Yes, I know. Sorry.'

'Only glad to help. I say, Imogen, am I allowed to know why he's so determined?' Drew's voice was wheedling.

'He's my husband, Drew.' Imogen frowned. 'Drew? Are you there?'

'Yes, I'm still here, Imogen. My God, it's a wonder he didn't kill me!' There was a pause. 'He has my sympathy. You really are a silly girl, you know,' but his voice was kind.

'I expect you're right. You won't let on, Drew, will you?'

'No. Ring me if you want me. 'Bye!'

As Imogen bathed and dressed she thought that perhaps she was a silly, but there was nothing she could do about it. A determined rap at the door heralded Nat's arrival and taking one look at his face, pale and tight-lipped, Imogen gathered together all her reserves of strength as she ushered him in.

'I suppose Wymark rang and told you I was coming?' A small nerve was jumping at the side of his jaw. 'Am I allowed to know why you asked him to help you?' His voice was quiet and controlled, but cut like a whiplash.

'It was better that way. Would you like some breakfast? The manager has been very kind.' As she poured out the coffee she asked: 'Have you found out anything more?'

'How can you be so calm, Imogen?'

'What do you want me to do?' she asked civilly. 'Hysterics won't bring him back. Here,' and she held out a cup to him.

'I feel as though I don't know you.'

'I don't think you ever have,' Imogen observed. 'When shall we know more?'

Nat looked at his watch. 'Half an hour. Less, perhaps.'

Imogen gazed at the breakfast tray and shuddered slightly. 'I don't think I can cope with the bacon and eggs. Can you? It would please the manager.'

'He'll have to be disappointed,' Nat said shortly, turning to stare out of the window, his back uncompromising.

'Did the party go well?' Imogen asked after a long pause, and Nat swung round, saying harshly:

'I don't know. I wasn't there. Good God, Imogen, if you think I could have attended that damned party . . .' He stopped, pressing his lips together.

'I don't see why not. Pa didn't mean anything to you, did he?' Imogen pointed out.

Nat stared at her, his face like sculptured stone. 'You twist the knife in my back, Imogen.'

She swallowed painfully. 'I don't mean to, Nat, truly.'

'Is it inconceivable that I might have been concerned for *you*? That *your* sorrow becomes *my own*? Do you not realise that I want to share your pain just as much as your joy?' He waited and she was silent. 'How do you think I felt when I found that Wymark was with you? That was when you put the knife into my back, Imogen,' and his voice was bitter with pain.

'You . . . have no need to fear Drew. He's only a friend,' she said, and he crossed the few yards between them, his voice gentling.

'You frighten me, Imogen, when I see you like this. Last night I could hardly believe you were real. To watch you, lighthearted and word-perfect, my beautiful Rosalind . . . my heart bled for you. And I was so proud of you, Imogen, as Gerard would have been. Oh, my very dear, dear love, it breaks my heart to see you like this, so frozen inside, so unnaturally composed. You *must* cry! It's not good for you to hold your grief back.' His arms enfolded her, his voice embracing her quietly like a warm cloak. 'Won't you let me comfort you, Imogen?' For a few moments he held her unresponsive body close and when he let her go, taking a pace back, his face was white and stricken.

Imogen gave a sad little smile. 'I'm sorry . . . I'm sorry, Nat. I need someone who loved Pa to comfort me. Please forgive me.'

He swung away, to stand hunched up by the window. Imogen wished she could comfort him, take away his hurt, but her limbs were heavy and she could not move.

A knock sounded on the door and a familiar voice called: 'Miss Imogen? Are you there?'

Imogen ran to it and threw it open and there stood Duggan. She went into his arms, and at last, the tears came.

CHAPTER EIGHT

'Come, woo me, woo me'

'So you see, Miss Adair, when the annuity for Mortimer Duggan is paid out, and the debts paid off, there will be very little left.' Mr Fisher stared at his client, a kindly, rather anxious expression on his face. 'You really cannot afford the annuity . . .'

'I have to afford it, Mr Fisher,' Imogen replied firmly. 'Duggan has been with my father for nearly twenty-five years and deserves some security in his old age.' She hesitated. 'I didn't realise that things were so bad.'

'No, I know. I did suggest to your father that perhaps it might be better for him to tell you, but, as you can appreciate, your father hoped things would look up, even though the signs were ominous as far back as five years ago.'

'So I'm practically penniless, am I?' joked Imogen, but her levity fell on stony ground.

'Ahem . . . you would, of course, be financially better off if you retained the sum of money that your . . . that Mr Beaumont has been paying into your account regularly,' and Mr Fisher looked hopeful.

'It must be returned.' Imogen spoke decisively. 'I allowed you to persuade me into letting him get us out of our present financial mess, but every penny has to be paid back.' She frowned. 'The Rover didn't make as much as I thought.'

'Second-hand cars depreciate in value, unfortunately, unless they are rare vintage models. If only your father had consulted Mr Beaumont when we first suggested it to him. The firm Sommers and Beaumont are well known in the City for having a firm grip on theatrical enterprises—it is their speciality. We have put work their way many times, and young Miss Sommers is due here later today, to meet one of our clients.'

'Miss Sommers?' Imogen pricked up her ears, suddenly interested.

Mr Fisher said: 'Yes, a sister, I believe, of Mr Sommers.'

'Is she late twenties, dark, and wears her hair taken back in a bun?'

Mr Fisher smiled. 'Yes, that's Miss Sommers. Do you know her?'

'I've seen her,' amended Imogen, remembering the attractive woman getting into Nat's car. A business meeting! She smiled warmly at Mr Fisher. 'I

understand Mr Beaumont has undertaken to find a
reputable director to take over the lease at
Norwich . . .'

'. . . on your behalf, Miss Adair, now that you are
your father's sole survivor. I'm afraid Mr Adair
would not have wished you to inherit so many debts
and a season of commitments, but he was always an
optimistic gentleman and, if I may say so, a great
loss to the theatre-going public.' Mr Fisher fiddled
with his paper-knife. 'Ahem . . . Mr Beaumont was
asking for your forwarding address.' He waited un-
happily, and Imogen was touched. Really, he was
such a dry old stick, who would have thought him to
be a romantic at heart? She stood up, holding out
her hand, saying smilingly:

'You've been very kind, Mr Fisher, and a great
help.' She was escorted to the door. 'I'll keep in
touch.'

'And Mr Beaumont?' he asked gently.

'Tell Mr Beaumont that there is no forwarding
address.'

'I see.' He picked up a brown paper parcel, flat
and square. 'He gave me this to give you.'

Imogen hesitated and took it.

Miss Dora Duggan lived in a small property in
the Palmers Green area of London, and it was there
that Imogen was staying until she decided what to
do with herself. Dora was a little older than her
brother, small and plump with plaited white hair
wound round her ears like headphones. She was
in direct contrast to Duggan's tall, magisterial bearing, but they were similar in their kindness to
Imogen.

Imogen let herself in to the house, the parcel Mr
Fisher had so surprisingly thrust upon her under her
arm. As she paused to hang her coat up in the hall,

voices came through the slightly ajar breakfast room door.

'I don't understand her. If she loves him and he loves her, why aren't they together, Mort? He's her husband and should be taking care of her at a time like this. What's he thinking of?'

Duggan's patient voice came back in answer. 'He wants to, Dora, but she won't let him yet.' The sound of crockery being placed on the table interrupted the next few words.

'. . . shouldn't be at all surprised if Sir didn't have something to do with the break-up in the first place.'

'Now, Dora, you shouldn't say that.'

'Maybe not. I know you won't have him criticised, and whenever I've met him he's been very kind and polite, but under that charm, Mort, there was steel for what he wanted, and don't you deny it.'

'I don't deny that he depended too much on Miss Imogen,' Duggan sounded uncomfortable, 'but Miss Imogen had a way with her that made it look as though he got his way, and I told Mr Beaumont that. Sir couldn't take her growing up and thinking for herself, that was the trouble, but she could cope with him.'

'What a way to go . . . and him being so set against aeroplanes! I just thank the dear Lord that you didn't go with him, Mort, that I do. Why did he go up in a flimsy thing like that? I've seen them on the television, nothing on them, look like toys, they do.'

'I've told you, Dora, it was for quickness' sake. He was offered this lift in a private plane, and there's nothing flimsy about them. Mr Gerard was always particular about being late for a performance and we'd been held up. It didn't matter me being late, so I went by train . . . and I've told you I don't want to talk about it.'

Dora sighed. 'I'm sorry, Mort. I know Sir meant a great deal to you, and he must have had something to have brought out all those crowds of people to his funeral. That great barn of a place—full, it was—and the television cameras there too.'

'St Paul's Church in Covent Garden is not a barn, Dora,' protested a horrified Duggan. 'It was built by Inigo Jones and many famous people are buried there, artists and such like. They call it the Actors' Church.'

'Really?' Dora sniffed. 'Well, to me it's still a great barn of a place, although I admit it's quite nice inside. Now, out of my way, Mort. Miss Imogen will be coming in soon. I must say she's looking better these last few days ... what a shock ...'

Imogen crept back to the front door, went out and came in again, banging the door loudly shut.

'I'm home,' she called, taking her time to hang her coat up, allowing them to change the subject. 'Mmm ... something smells good,' she announced, walking in. She kissed them both on the cheek. 'Good news—I've got a job!'

'Where, Miss Imogen?' Duggan asked anxiously.

'Remember I told you about Jake Edwards—the *Arts Diary* man? I found his card the other day and gave him a ring. He has a hand in producing commercials for television and he's got me a small part in one coming up next week. Very small and not difficult, but the pay's good.'

'Fancy! Television!' Dora bustled into the kitchen, and Imogen smiled at Duggan as they heard the awe in her voice.

'Shall you be in London, then, Miss Imogen?'

'Wherever I am, I shall keep in touch, Duggan, you know I will. You're the only link I have left with Pa.'

'And will you keep in touch with Mr Nat?' Duggan asked stubbornly.

'Duggan, I can't explain,' she blurted out. 'I'm . . . not ready.'

'Mind you don't leave it too late, that's all. He's a good man, is Mr Nat, and he's waited long enough.' Duggan coughed, ears pink with embarrassment. 'Begging your pardon, Miss Imogen.'

Imogen crossed and put her arms round him. 'It will be all right, I promise you. I have to prove something to myself, Duggan.' Her eyes fell on the parcel and she began to untie it.

'Now that's what I call a nice picture,' Duggan remarked approvingly when she held it up. He peered closer. 'You can almost pick the grass, it's so real. Rather a deserted place, though, Miss Imogen. Do you know it?'

Imogen nodded, saying absently: 'Yes, it's part of the Norfolk coast.'

'Ah—near where Mr Nat lives, perhaps?'

Imogen turned her eyes from the picture and looked thoughtfully at Duggan, asking casually: 'You've had one or two chats with Nat recently?'

Duggan set his face in stubborn lines. 'Yes, I have, Miss Imogen, and he wants to see you. To have a talk.'

'I know he does,' she replied gently, re-tying the parcel, and puzzled, Duggan said uncertainly: 'I thought the picture was a present,' and she gave a wry smile.

'More like a message, Duggan, and it has to be returned. Poor Mr Fisher *will* be disappointed,' and on that cryptic note Duggan had to be content.

Sadie rang, saying she would be in London the following day and could Imogen meet her for lunch. They arranged to see each other in Leicester Square.

Imogen was early. The Square was a good meeting place for people making up their minds where to go, what to do ... the mass of eating and drinking places and the brash cinema advertisements all fighting with each other to tempt.

In the enclosed garden of the Square, however, it was possible to shut off the surrounding buildings and thronging crowds. It was a lovely day. The plane trees and the statue of Shakespeare, the water basin and stone dolphins, the strutting pigeons, all took on a very pleasant aspect in the sunshine.

Imogen glanced at her watch and thought, Sadie is late, and her eyes swung round the garden to the entrances, seeking a glimpse of her friend, anticipating her apologetic grin.

It was not Sadie who stood watching her, but Nat. He held her startled glance for a moment and then came forward, slowing to a halt a couple of yards away, his face austere.

Imogen said: 'I suppose Sadie arranged this?' discovering that she had not lost her powers of speech, after all. So long as she did not look at him her mind would remain reasonably clear, her resolve too. She heard the slight smile in his voice as he replied:

'Yes. Sadie is a romantic. Would you like to go somewhere for coffee?'

'No, thank you.'

'Are you going to let me be part of your life, Imogen?'

Hunger at his nearness was almost unbearable. She had been right to refuse to meet him. It was much, much worse than she had imagined. 'Can't you see that everything's changed, Nat?' she burst out desperately, and he replied grimly:

'The fact that I love you and you love me hasn't changed. That has never altered. We might have strayed off the path a little through circumstances and our own and other people's inadequacies, but whatever else, that remains. Hasn't it?' When she did not speak, he went on doggedly: 'Won't you, at least, sit and talk for a while?' His mouth twisted. 'You're quite safe in broad daylight with half London looking on.'

Imogen was not so sure. The sight and sound of him was desperately unnerving, but they could not stand here any longer, there was an old woman on one of the seats showing great curiosity. Imogen said in an undertone:

'Only if you promise not to be angry. I . . . can't bear it when you're angry.'

'I promise I'll try,' he said soothingly, unable to keep the tiny spurt of triumph from his voice or his bearing as he took her arm, leading her to a vacant seat. The pigeons scattered before them as they walked. Once seated, Nat gazed at her steadily, bringing the colour to her cheeks. 'You're looking very beautiful, Imogen,' he said at last, his lips curving into a fleeting smile as he saw the alarm in her eyes. 'I've only promised not to be angry, and said nothing about making love to you.'

'Nat, please . . .'

The smile deepened. 'There are limitations imposed in such a public place, I agree, but it's surprising what you can achieve if you're determined enough.' He paused. 'And I am a very determined man, Imogen, my love. You may look away, but you know when I take your hand, like this, and look at you, as I'm doing now, that I'm making love to you.'

Imogen rallied her reserves and said steadily: 'Why did you want to see me, Nat?'

'Very well. I'll be good, for the moment.' He

leaned forward, arms resting on his knees, studying the ground at his feet, marshalling his thoughts. When he at last spoke, his voice took on a matter-of-fact tone. 'Do you know why I'm consumed with anger, Imogen? The slow-burning, helpless kind? Because your father looks like winning. His death has put the final barrier between us and we'll be fools if we allow that barrier to stay.' He took her hands between his, searching her face. 'None of us is perfect, my dear. Sometimes our faults come as a surprise to us. I was an arrogant fool, three years ago. My pride took a tremendous knock and the way I behaved sits heavily upon my conscience . . .'

'Nat, I must tell you . . .'

'Please—let me finish, it's important that you understand, Imogen, and confession is good for the soul.' He gave a short, derisive laugh. 'Nat Beaumont, for years coolly and methodically organising his life, fell deeply in love at long last and became someone no longer in control of either himself or his destiny! I was as jealous of Gerard's hold over you as he was of mine. I'm not proud of the fact, Imogen, I can only plead that emotionally I was off balance . . . I behaved like a fool, issuing ultimatums all over the place . . .'

'You were not to know . . .'

'Exactly. We can all fall back on the fact that we don't know the whole. It's as good an excuse as any. So . . . we agree that none of us is perfect.' He rubbed a finger absently along her wrist, frowning slightly. 'My furthest wish is to hurt you any more than you already have been, but we must have the truth between us. Gerard was jealous and possessive to extraordinary lengths, but I knew, and so did you, Imogen . . .' he paused and green eyes commanded grey ones, '. . . my dear, we knew that had he lived, had he come home, we should have found some way to reconcile him to us being together. Wouldn't we?'

'Yes.' A whisper, but he was satisfied.

'It was unspoken between us, but we knew and we sealed that knowledge the night you stayed with me . . . didn't we?'

Imogen took a deep breath. 'Yes, Nat, we did.' Her voice was dull and lifeless. 'And Pa's death wouldn't have changed anything, I only needed a breathing space . . .'

'So why are we sitting here, with a yard of seat between us? Why are we here in the first place and not at home, at Caffrey's, where we belong?' Nat demanded harshly, and Imogen broke in:

'Because everything's changed!'

'In what way?'

'Last night I was clearing Pa's trunk and found his deedbox. It didn't hold much, some old photographs, birth certificates, things like that,' she blurted out in a rush, not daring to look at him, 'and at the bottom . . . were two letters. The two you wrote when you were in Australia.'

'I see.'

'He hadn't opened them. I didn't know you'd written.' She pulled her hands away and covered her face. 'So you see, you have every right to be angry.'

Nat sat back, his arms resting along the seat. There was a long, long silence and he said at last: 'You've read them?' and when she nodded, he mused: 'I admit to being very bitter when you ignored them. I threw myself into my work as if it were a lifeline, which it was, in a way. I kidded myself that I was well rid of you . . . that you no longer meant anything to me. I came back to England, glad that Adam had a job for me, I needed work, because I found I'd lost the capacity to play. The minute I saw you all the anger and bitterness welled up inside and I wanted to hurt you. It wasn't long before I realised that I was only hurting myself.' He took her hands once more, smoothing their tensed grip until they lay between his palms. 'I'm glad you found them, glad that you know I wrote . . . but it really changes nothing.'

She turned her eyes on him, bright with tears. 'How can you say that, Nat? I thought you'd be so angry when I told you. What Pa did to you was a terrible thing!'

'Nothing is changed,' Nat repeated firmly. 'We're three years older and wiser, Imogen. I know that if you'd received those letters you would have replied, would have come to me eventually.' He paused and she said painfully:

'Yes, I would have come.'

'Even after Zoe.'

'Even after . . .' She eyed him hopelessly, wondering if she would ever cope with his quirky sense of humour, the frozen mass round her heart beginning to melt as she saw the glimmer of gentle, loving amusement dancing in his eyes. 'I didn't blame you. I was a fool too. I deserved Zoe,' she answered fiercely, and Nat threw back his head and laughed deep in his throat.

'That's remarkably magnanimous of you, my love, and grinds my own faults deep in the dust. I'm afraid I can't be so forgiving where Drew Wymark is concerned.'

'You know that Drew was nothing but a friend,' Imogen protested. 'I feel badly about Drew.'

'And so you should, poor fellow!'

'You're not trying to tell me that Zoe was just a

friend,' she went on indignantly, and Nat, wonderfully mild, ventured:

'I only admit to "living it up with the boys" for three days running when you left, wallowing in self-pity and misery. Zoe dug me out of my squalor and administered to my revolting needs, sobering me up enough to catch the plane out to Australia. A good friend, is Zoe.' He slanted her a glance. 'If I'd wanted to marry her, I would have done so years ago.' He lifted her hand to his cheek, despite the interest of the old woman transfixed to her seat, turning the palm to his lips. 'Even after Zoe, you would have come to me, would you? And you have the nerve to say that it's all over between us!' and the look in his eyes brought a confused agitation to her breast.

Imogen made a feeble attempt to free her hand, and in a voice that did not seem to belong to her, said: '*You* can forgive Pa, but the dreadful thing is, Nat, I don't think I can.'

'I can teach you how to,' he said simply, and she shook her head. Nat heaved a sigh. 'Very well, you can have time, Imogen, but don't keep me waiting too long, will you? I'm not a patient man, I've found.' He laughed quietly, a finger coming up to smooth a lock of hair falling against her flushed cheek. 'I shall use fair means and foul to bring you to your senses,' he added, in the deep, gentle voice that was so unnerving her.

She looked at him then, seeing a mixture of love and exasperation on his face.

'It would be easy to come back to you now, Nat. I have to prove something, to myself and, in a way, to you too.' She rose to her feet, saying softly, appealingly: 'You do understand?'

'I'll try to.' Nat stood up. 'When you've proved

that you can stand on your own two feet, Imogen—
a fact which I know you're quite capable of—let me
know.'

She gave a wonky smile and he took her left hand
and held it between them. 'I want my ring putting
back on this finger—do you understand?' His voice
thickened. 'You'd better go now, before I forget
where we are. Go on—scoot!'

Imogen's heart turned a silly somersault at the
expression on his face and gathering herself together
she broke away and walked quickly until she was
lost in the crowd.

Nat stood watching her, a brooding air about his
stance. The old woman caught his eye and he smiled
wryly at her before turning on his heel and going
rapidly in the opposite direction.

Imogen did three commercials in all with Jake
Edwards, each one a little more involved, and then
her agent rang to see if she was interested in a
month's contract with the Theatre in Education in
Nottinghamshire. She said she was and found that
she enjoyed working with children, that improvisa-
tion was a 'must' and that one needed superhuman
stamina.

The postcards, forwarded by Mr Fisher, arrived
at her lodgings at regular intervals. The first was of
Queensbridge University and campus. The words
'Wish you were here' were written across the back in
Nat's handwriting. The second was a picture of
Tower Bridge and the Thames, and the words
'Working hard, are you?' brought a smile to her lips.
There was a longer gap and Imogen spent a desper-
ate few days until the next one came, of Norwich
Cathedral, with the words 'Working hard, missing
you—how much longer?'

Not much longer, thought Imogen, counting the days to the end of her contract. On the first day of her freedom she went to Queensbridge and Treetops for the weekend, and Liz and Adam welcomed her warmly. Liz asked no questions, but was reassured by Imogen's serenity. After tea on Sunday she made a great show of reading the paper and exclaiming:

'Hey, you two! Tonight it's the *Arts Diary* profile on Nat! We must watch,' and she observed the swift blush to Imogen's cheeks with quiet satisfaction, while Adam looked at his wife with loving amusement.

Imogen fought for composure as the time arrived and the pleasant face of Jake Edwards came on to the screen, and she was glad of the dimly lit room. As the programme unfolded, and scenes of *As You Like It*, both in rehearsal and on stage, were shown, she thought how strange it was, 'seeing oneself as others see us' and was faintly surprised and not a little pleased. She really did make rather a nice boy, she decided complacently. But her whole being was concerned with Nat, her eyes never wavering.

What on earth am I doing, sitting here, watching him on the screen when I could be sitting being held in his arms? she wailed inwardly with an impatience born out of foolishness. With a pang she realised that the programme was nearly finished and she watched and listened hungrily as Jake gave the final interview with Nat in person.

'I understand that you're returning to Australia at the end of this year,' Jake was saying, and Imogen sat frozen in her chair, eyes widely fixed on the set.

Nat smiled and nodded an admission. 'Yes, that's correct. I shall be filming, in conjunction with Australian television, a story about an English girl who travels out to Australia to marry a man she's never met, only corresponded with, and the difficulties she has of adapting to a strange country. It's set in the Outback, written by an Australian, and all the actors and actresses will be Australian.'

Jake leaned forward, interested. 'Other than the English girl.'

'Yes, of course,' and Nat grinned while Jake assumed a poker face.

'I believe this will be something of a pleasure for you, Nat, in that you'll be working with your wife.'

Nat now smiled broadly. 'That's right. She will be playing the English girl, Grace Armstrong.'

Jake looked as though he was enjoying himself. 'We've just seen her, have we not, playing Rosalind in the production you directed at Queensbridge of *As You Like It*. Imogen Adair, daughter of the late Gerard Adair. When shall we be able to see this Australian epic?'

'This time next year, probably. It will be released to the television networks over here in serial form.'

The few seconds dealing with the winding up of the programme were missed by the fact that Liz bounded to her feet, crying:

'Oh, clever, clever Nat! To force your hand so publicly, Imogen!' and she dragged Imogen up and waltzed her round while Adam watched them, smiling.

Imogen gave a laugh, her face rueful. 'He said he'd use fair means or foul.' She turned to Adam, Liz's arms still affectionately round her. 'How long have you known?'

Adam rose and switched the television set off, saying: 'Not until that first day of rehearsal, when I officially handed over to Beau, who felt that I ought to be told.'

'Adam! Really?' quizzed Liz, adding plaintively:

'I might have known . . . and neither of us split on you. How's that for loyalty, Imogen?'

Imogen hugged her hard. 'You're dears and I love you both.'

'Isn't it about time you said the same thing to Beau?' asked Adam teasingly, and Imogen smiled and said simply: 'Yes, it is.'

The bus rolled down the winding lanes, the heat rising up, stirring the dust. Imogen sat near an open window, enjoying the breeze on her face, absently twisting the wedding ring she was now wearing on her finger. She sniffed the air enthusiastically, sure she could smell the sea.

Alighting at a crossroads, she set off down the lane, the July sun gloriously hot on her bare arms and legs. A sudden awful thought nearly stopped her in her tracks. Was she being absurdly optimistic sending a postcard? Suppose it had been lost in the post? Suppose . . . oh, thousands of dreadful things might have happened to it! Lulu might even have eaten it! Aghast, she quickened her steps, eager to have her fears made laughable, and a hundred yards would either confirm them or . . .

She rounded the curve in the track and was almost blinded by the glare of the sun striking the bright chrome and brilliant red bodywork of the Ferrari.

Imogen stopped and caught her breath, relief flooding through her, and her mouth broke out into a joyful smile. The dear, darling postcard had arrived safely! Three rousing cheers for the postman! She touched the Ferrari almost lovingly as she passed by. How clever of Nat to bring it . . . he was going back, right to the very beginning.

She crossed the soft sand of the dunes and stood, high up, the breeze lifting her hair, the marram grass flicking her legs while her eyes swept the panorama of the coastline.

It was deserted, as usual. This stretch of coast was too difficult an access for most holidaymakers. Only the very persistent, determined on privacy, attained this beach.

A dark, moving object came from the dunes farther along, bounding down to the sea. Imogen laughed, running down the slope of the dune, scattering sandals and bag as she went.

Lulu lifted her head, hearing her name on the breeze, and began to bounce towards her. Their meeting was joyful and boisterous for a few minutes and then they began to walk back along the shore, both paddling in the shallow water at the edge.

The solitary figure standing on the top of the dune, a few yards from the discarded sandals, was reminded vividly of his painting, and shielding the sun from his eyes, watched their progress as they came near.

When Imogen lifted her eyes and saw him she felt her heart beating near to suffocation, and she stopped, her body poised, motionless.

Unaware that she had moved, Imogen found herself running towards him as Nat strode down the side of the dune, gaining momentum until they were in each other's arms and he was twirling her round and round before kissing her fiercely, triumphantly.

When they came to a dizzy, laughing halt Imogen pulled at his hair with mock anger. 'Oh, how could you, Nat Beaumont! On television in front of hundreds of viewers!'

Nat grinned. 'I told you I wasn't going to wait long. When Jake sent for me to do the final interview we set it up between us. Then I made sure you'd be seeing the programme via Adam and Liz, and hey presto . . .!'

'Blackmail,' reproached Imogen, murmuring into his chest: 'I was ready to give in—honestly.'

'I'm very glad to hear it.' They stood for a moment, content to smile into each other's eyes before Nat turned his head to the sea, gauging the tide. 'Shall we swim before we eat? Rosa has packed us a picnic.'

'Mmm . . . sounds lovely,' agreed Imogen, her eyes brimming mischievously, '. . . for starters.'

Tingling from her battle with the North Sea waves, Imogen lay on the sand, arms spread to the sun. A shadow loomed across her closed lids and she opened her eyes to find Nat smiling lazily at her, scattering droplets of water as his head bent down to hers.

'You taste salty,' she said breathlessly.

'You . . . taste . . . delicious.' Each word was punctuated by a longer and longer kiss, until Nat asked softly: 'Shall we go home?' and Imogen nodded, suddenly feeling ridiculously shy.

Home! What a lovely word that was—when home meant Nat.

Caffrey's had not changed, it was still as mellow and even more beautiful, backed as it was with trees in summer leaf and the garden in full flower. The watercolour painting was back on the wall where it belonged, the horses were safe in the stables and Lulu was asleep on the step. Imogen walked each room lovingly, her heart full of happiness.

Coming down the stairs she heard Nat on the telephone and leaning over the banister she traced his profile with a finger, her hand caught and imprisoned while he talked.

'Yes, Adam, we shall come, of course. On the

twenty-fifth.' Nat listened, smiling up at Imogen, murmuring a 'yes' here and there, and Imogen kissed the back of his neck tantalisingly.

When he finished Nat swung her down the remaining stairs, saying: 'That, as you must have gathered, was Adam. He and Liz want us to come to the end-of-season do at the Queen's. I've said yes.'

Imogen pulled a comical face. 'Oh, lord! How shall I face everyone?'

'As my wife,' retorted Nat with ferocious authority. He cocked his head, listening intently. 'That's Lulu whining to go out. Shall we walk her in the garden before turning in?'

Imogen murmured her agreement and went to collect a cardigan. She joined Nat outside as he stood with his face turned to the stars.

'Mmm ... what a lovely night—and doesn't everywhere smell nice?' With a little sigh of contentment, she slipped beneath his protecting arm and they began to walk slowly along the path, Lulu a dark shadow darting here and there. When they reached the gate at the end of the drive they turned as one and leaned back against it.

Imogen said suddenly: 'Nat—you didn't really think I was falling for Adam, did you?' She tilted him a glance, taking in his profile a mite anxiously. 'I've loved Adam all my life, but it's certainly not the same kind of love that I feel for you.'

Nat ran his fingers through her hair, cupping the back of her neck. 'I know.' He gave a gentle laugh. 'I knew then, but I'm afraid you made me say and do many things that were governed by pure frustration ... and it's quite possible for a girl your age to fall for an older man. Adam's only forty-four and damned attractive. In my darker moments I could see you turning to him.'

Imogen touched his face delicately. 'Adam has and always will be a good friend, and he's never seen me in any other light than the daughter of an older man who befriended him in his youth.' She paused, thinking deeply, saying presently: 'I've come to terms, made my peace with Pa, Nat. I've ... learned to love him again, accept him for what he was.'

Nat kissed her gently. 'I'm glad. Remember, he must have been a lonely man. I'm glad you can think of him again with affection.'

Imogen shivered and Nat, his voice concerned, asked quickly: 'Cold?'

She shook her head and lifted her face to the outline of the house, its gables etched against the sky.

'No, not cold. I was thinking how happy I am ... how much I love you.'

Nat tightened his hold but did not speak. They began to walk slowly back towards the house.

'Nat, do you think we could have a cat some time?'

'I don't see why not.'

'Poor Poss!' They walked a few more paces and she said dreamily: 'Children ought to have animals around the place ... a hamster, and a rabbit and perhaps a guineapig. And there'll be the horses too.' She turned her face to his. 'How does that sound to you?'

'Crowded,' said Nat. 'You say children. Are you holding out on me?'

Imogen teased: 'That would spoil all your plans of hauling me off to the Aussie Outback, wouldn't it?'

'Not at all. One of my fair means was hoping that our stolen night together might solve all my problems.'

She laughed softly. 'I wondered myself ... but no, I'm not holding out on you. Not yet. But when we do have a baby, Nat, I hope I can give you a daughter. Somehow, I feel you might think more kindly about Pa ...' She stopped and mentally shook herself, giving a wobbly laugh. 'Doesn't the house look solid and dependable with the warm light from the sitting room shining out to greet us?'

Nat murmured an agreement, saying: 'You're getting chilled—let's go in.' When she made no move to go, he asked, puzzled: 'What is it?'

'Nothing. We can go now.' Imogen saw him smile and shake his head slightly, pandering to her, not understanding. They trod the path, the air heavy with the scent of roses, Nat giving a low whistle to call Lulu to his side. She felt the firmness of his grasp and knew that she was not only talking about the house. Nat was solid and dependable too. He took her hand, threading it through his arm, and led her inside.

We value your opinion...

You can help us make our books even better by completing and mailing this questionnaire. Please check [√] the appropriate boxes.

1. Compared to romance series by other publishers, do Harlequin novels have any additional features that make them more attractive?

   1.1 ☐ yes   .2 ☐ no   .3 ☐ don't know

   If yes, what additional features? _____
   _____
   _____

2. How much do these additional features influence your purchasing of Harlequin novels?

   2.1 ☐ a great deal   .2 ☐ somewhat   .3 ☐ not at all   .4 ☐ not sure

3. Are there any other additional features you would like to include?

   _____
   _____
   _____

4. Where did you obtain this book?

   4.1 ☐ bookstore   .4 ☐ borrowed or traded
     .2 ☐ supermarket   .5 ☐ subscription
     .3 ☐ other store   .6 ☐ other (please specify)_____

5. How long have you been reading Harlequin novels?

   5.1 ☐ less than 3 months   .4 ☐ 1-3 years
     .2 ☐ 3-6 months   .5 ☐ more than 3 years
     .3 ☐ 7-11 months   .6 ☐ don't remember

6. Please indicate your age group.

   6.1 ☐ younger than 18   .3 ☐ 25-34   .5 ☐ 50 or older
     .2 ☐ 18-24   .4 ☐ 35-49

Please mail to: **Harlequin Reader Service**

In U.S.A.	In Canada
1440 South Priest Drive	649 Ontario Street
Tempe, AZ 85281	Stratford, Ontario N5A 6W2

Thank you very much for your cooperation.

Harlequin Presents...

**Stories to dream about...
Stories of love...**

...all-consuming, passionate love,
the way you've always imagined it,
the way you know it should be!

FREE!

A hardcover Romance Treasury volume
containing 3 treasured works of romance
by 3 outstanding Harlequin authors...

...as your introduction to Harlequin's
Romance Treasury subscription plan!

...almost 600 pages of exciting romance reading
every month at the low cost of $6.97 a volume!

A wonderful way to collect many of Harlequin's most beautiful love
stories, all originally published in the late '60s and early '70s.
Each value-packed volume, bound in a distinctive gold-embossed
leatherette case and wrapped in a colorfully illustrated dust jacket,
contains...
• 3 full-length novels by 3 world-famous authors of romance fiction
• a unique illustration for every novel
• the elegant touch of a delicate bound-in ribbon bookmark...
  and much, much more!

Romance Treasury

...for a library of romance you'll treasure forever!

Complete and mail today the FREE gift certificate and subscription
reservation on the following page.

Romance Treasury

An exciting opportunity to collect treasured works of romance! Almost 600 pages of exciting romance reading in each beautifully bound hardcover volume!

You may cancel your subscription whenever you wish! You don't have to buy any minimum number of volumes. Whenever you decide to stop your subscription just drop us a line and we'll cancel all further shipments.